King's Mercy

Colin Fletcher

Grosvenor House
Publishing Limited

This book is published by
Grosvenor House Publishing Ltd
Link House
140 The Broadway, Tolworth, Surrey, KT6 7HT.
www.grosvenorhousepublishing.co.uk

This book is a work of fiction. Any resemblance to
people or events, past or present, is purely coincidental.

A CIP record for this book
is available from the British Library

ISBN 978-1-80381-062-1

CONTENTS

ACKNOWLEDGEMENTS

I have used an extract from *The Canterbury Tales*; 'Here beginnith the Nonne Preestes Tale of the Cok and Hen, Chauntecleer and Pertelote'.

Chaucer provides a contemporary picture of a poor widow's living conditions late in the fourteenth century that is just too tempting to resist, and I have used this in Chapter Three. The widow is dwelling in a narrow cottage with two rooms, beside a grove, standing in a dale.

No wine drank she, neither white nor red,
Her bord was served most with whyt and blak,
Milk and broun breed, in which she found no lak,
... A yard she hadde, enclosed all aboute
With stikkes, and a dry dich with-oute,
In which she hadde a cok, hight Chauntecleer,
In al the land of crowing nas his peer.

Chaucer himself is encountered on the London Wool Wharf in Chapter Four of *King's Mercy*, where Cedric notices an older man with long white hair, though also with surprisingly dark eyebrows. Paul Strohm explains the background in *The Poet's Tale*; formerly at Court, Chaucer's varied career had fluctuated in the face of events beyond his control. Now the great players had placed him as controller of wool exports, potentially generating one third of the king's income; here he was serving some of the greediest men in the city of London.

Edith, eldest daughter of the Johnson family, had long been head of the family, and her funeral in Chapter Six drew a large congregation to the church at Compton near Calne, since called Compton Bassett. The development of the Norman Church has been traced by John Chandler and Derek Parker, authors of *The Church in Wiltshire*, and provides valuable help in understanding the condition of the village church in the late fourteenth century.

The Characters.

Edith Johnson: eldest daughter of John and Joan. Like her brothers, she was taught to write her name by her father, writing 'Edith, son of John'; this later simplified to 'Johnson'. Born during the famine years, she had been stunted by malnutrition, as had her brother, born one year later.

Charles the clothier: the younger son of a younger son of a landowning family. He had inherited no land but established a weaving business near Bridgewater. He expanded his interests to weaving and marketing in Salisbury, the rapidly growing cloth trade capital of southern England.

A poor widow: twenty years after this period, Chaucer provided a contemporary description of a poor widow in *The Canterbury Tales*. The life of just such another poor widow struggling to deal with the loss of a husband and a son during the violence at Bridgewater reveals the personal misery of an historic event.

Emma: eldest daughter of the poor widow, works in Bridgewater and often frequents the harbour where she enjoys meeting sailors and visitors to the town.

Cedric Johnson: nephew of Edith and the eldest son of **Morris** from *White Clyffe*. A few miles north of Calne, he had been caught up in the excitement of meetings across Wiltshire campaigning for better conditions. A group of enthusiasts moving from town to town arrived at Salisbury in large numbers, to the alarm of the military. Cedric was one among many who simply disappeared.

Peronell (Nell) Johnson: sister to Cedric and niece to Edith, moves to Salisbury and forms an attachment to Charles.

Ethel: wife of Charles the clothier. She and Albert the foreman recover the Bridgewater cloth mill, supported by infrequent visits from Charles.

PROLOGUE by Cedric Johnson.

After a few years at sea, it was wonderful to return to White Clyffe and see Father again, still strong and sharp, yet Mother already frail and weak. But soon I came to know I no longer belonged there. Too much had happened.

The danger, for one thing. I was a marked man; already arrested, interrogated in Salisbury then press ganged into the king's fighting ship at Southampton. Stowed away on an English freighter, travelling across the seas, I soon felt that was the safest place.

And the smell of the sea gets to you after a while. It is a purer and fresher air. And there is nothing to match the quiver of a wooden deck that comes best through naked feet. The lovely old ship, she strains and heaves through endless waves, punished by wind and sail.

CHAPTER ONE

A Tale of Late Love.

Edith might have slipped gently into old age, knitting pretty woollens for her grandchildren, but her brain would not let her; her brain was a hard, muscular organ, trained and toned by decades of anxiety. Her journeys to Salisbury became more frequent and lasted longer. Her friendship for the kind and talkative man developed quickly, and overnight visits were often extended by two or three days, while her sons were no longer alarmed by her delayed return.

Her purchases of imported wines and smart clothes that could not be obtained in the country towns sold quickly, so the boys were always glad to receive each new wagonload. A three-way discussion on the cost of the new purchases established the attempted selling prices, and all this had to be carried in the head.

"Don't leave that old stuff on the shelf, mind. Get rid of it at the best price you can."

"Yes, Mother."

"I don't know why it is still here."

"Well, you bought the wrong stuff that time."

She started, shocked by the criticism, but sorted through the slow movers, determined not to repeat the mistake.

"Will you be staying long before you go back to Salisbury?"

"Oh, I'll just have a tidy up at home. And I need to see if the sheep are all right. Are you keeping an eye on them?"

"Most days we see them. But they won't be lambing yet. Then we shall need you to be here a bit longer."

The brothers grinned behind her back, but Edith ignored the remark.

Six weeks later, she warned her friend that lambing was approaching and she might be missing for a few weeks. His face fell, then brightened with a new thought.

"I could come with you and maybe help with the lambing. I used to do it years ago."

She turned to his smiling face and hugged him.

"I'd really like that. It's time you met the boys."

Edith now had more time to explore the city; she was no longer rushing to buy supplies and hurrying to return to Calne, as she had for so many years. The city was almost tranquil, away from the busiest streets and the dreadful weaving shops. A number of chalk streams entered the main river within Salisbury, and she knew nothing more soothing than clear, flowing water.

One afternoon, Edith was sure she saw the man with the pleasant voice who had helped her search for Cedric, but if he recognised her, he made no sign of it. He was busy talking to two other people, and she made no attempt to interrupt them.

There was still an active military presence, although the rebellion had been crushed. Yet there had been no violence in Salisbury, unlike in some of the other towns. Edith often wondered what they had done with Cedric and where they were keeping him. Was he even still alive? Should she see the people who tried to help her before, or would that be too dangerous? She could not decide what she might do. Perhaps she should just wait and hope. It would be nice to get back to her sheep and concentrate on the new-born lambs again.

If she was busy again, it might put her mind at rest. Edith decided to speak to Harry and see how soon she could leave Salisbury, with him beside her.

Three days later, they were heading out of Salisbury, along the Avon Valley towards Amesbury, happy to be together, and with no thought of Cedric. At Upavon they struck west, keeping to the southern edge of the Pewsey Vale, Edith's heart warmed by the sight of the Marlborough Downs again, though her hands were chilled by the crisp March air. This was all new to Harry, and he enjoyed the villages beyond Amesbury and the rugged hills a few miles across the broad fertile valley of Pewsey. As Edith pointed out the farms and villages she had known for so many decades and recalled the families of long ago, she may have wondered how many more times she might travel this road. Whether from this thought, or the bracing spring air, she shivered and slid closer to Harry on the hard wooden bench, seeking his comforting warmth.

Within a few days, the first lamb was born, and they were too busy for reflection. The lambs must have their mother's milk quickly for inner warmth, and they must be licked and pummelled dry, even before they could stand. Any ewe that looked to be close to lambing must be kept away from the March wind overnight. Hurdles were fixed up hurriedly so that if several ewes lambed together, all might be safe. In extreme circumstances, sickly lambs might be brought into the little house that was always cluttered with possessions and a muddle from one wall to the other.

Severe storms and high winds were a particular worry, and soaking cold rain as damaging as snow. New lambs under a clear sky on a still, frosty night were less of a worry, and the night patrols were much less of an ordeal.

After a succession of busy nights, Edith and Harry were exhausted, snatching a brief sleep whenever possible; perhaps for longer in the warmth of the middle of the day. They lay together, limbs entwined for comfort, maybe counting the number of lambs they had brought into the world. When one stirred, the other woke, too.

Not knowing how long they had slept, they jumped up guiltily. Edith poked the fire and Harry went out for some more sticks; the sun had gone behind a thick cloud, and a bitter wind blew from the east.

"We better go round the main lot of ewes, Harry. We can look at the new lambs when we come back. I'll just make the fire up; we'll want a hot drink when we come in."

They went out into the paddock behind the house. Fine grains of dry snow stung their faces like grit, flying horizontally till reaching a hedge or a thicket. Falling to the ground, the snow soon formed a small heap that would become a large drift in a few hours. The ewes were sheltering from the wind where they could, not yet troubled by the cold through their thick woollen coats.

"We'll bring them out some hay before dark, Harry. They won't eat much otherwise."

Returning to the yard, they checked the new-born lambs and put some hay out for the mothers. Harry thought it would be a good idea to prepare some more hurdles in case they were needed in a hurry. Later he carried hay to the main flock, but the ewes would not leave the shelter of the hedge, so he put it close beside them. The snow was blowing into drifts as he returned, and he thought they would have a difficult night.

Edith had a hard head for business, but she had milked her flock of twenty ewes for many years and remembered the mothers and grandmothers of them all; she cared for them now as they were threatened by bitter weather.

Throughout that long night, Edith and Harry returned again and again to two ewes who were close to lambing. The first ewe was older and seemed quite weak. The lamb had to be helped out while the old ewe lay flat, too exhausted to stir. Edith rubbed the lamb quite briskly with some dry straw. Next, she drew some milk, squirting it over the lamb's mouth and most of its head, then pushed the teat firmly into the lamb's mouth. The milk was not as warm as normal, and it was increasingly clear that the poor old ewe had died.

Edith passed the lamb to Harry and drew as much milk as she could into a bowl. Returning to the house, they laid the lamb beside the fire, and when the milk had been warmed, placed a soaked cloth in its mouth, hoping the lamb would get some benefit.

An hour later, they found that the other ewe had made better progress, and her lamb was already sucking. Edith hurried back to pick up the weak lamb. She took it to the new mother, rubbing its head and body in the fresh afterbirth, which the ewe had not yet eaten. Then she fastened the lamb's head onto the foster mother's teat and did not rest till the lamb sucked strongly. Once more, she rubbed it with the afterbirth to disguise its alien smell and lay it beside the other lamb.

Later in the night, Edith was delighted to see the ewe up on her feet, and both lambs sucking side by side. She returned to the house and slept heavily till first light.

Harry had just returned from the yard and poked up the fire, a trail of snowy footprints slowly turning to small puddles.

As she stirred, he said, "Both doin' well."

Edith nodded comfortably. "I thought they would."

CHAPTER TWO

Wreckage.

Between May and December, the young king and his advisors had been very frightened indeed, for they had experienced the first dangerous and effective rebellion in the period of known English history. Local unrest was commonplace, but rebellion on a national scale was quite unknown. Once the stopper was out of the barrel, could they ever get it back in again?

Ever since the Black Death, the poorest villagers and town dwellers had gradually become aware of their growing strength. With every wave of bubonic plague, the availability of labourers was reduced, and the shortage of workers became more acute. But the organisation of the revolt in Kent and Essex depended on the skills and confidence of small business people and independent farmers in pastoral areas; their speeches and rallying calls were the sparks that ignited the spontaneous rage of the masses.

The targets were precise and repeated in the northern and western counties, even after the death of Wat Tyler and the crushing of the first uprising. The greediest amassers of wealth had been identified, and their houses burned. Church leaders among them were not spared; an archbishop had been dragged from his cathedral to an open place and had his head hacked off unsatisfactorily with a blunt knife.

Legal records were identified as a particular threat to owners of businesses and property, if not the labourer, and were burnt in a number of separate violent incidents suggesting a coherent strategy.

Rage was the drug that conquered the young king's fear; outrage at lower class impertinence sustained the unequal contest and the bloody slaughter from London to Yorkshire and from Kent to Somerset. But even after many months of retribution, the administration remained deeply insecure.

Intelligent people who had recognised the inefficiencies and waste and feared the working-class fury also understood the continued threat of local spies and informers. Charles the clothier knew this danger and had resisted the agonising temptation to return to his abandoned business near Bridgewater. He wondered how his workers had survived, how many had been killed or imprisoned, yet could not risk a connection between his broken business in Bridgewater and his current activities in Salisbury.

Towards the end of the year, military activity appeared to decline in southern England, and Charles began to wonder if he might risk a visit to Bridgewater, but then he thought perhaps not yet. His simple business in Salisbury was quite satisfactory. He bought wool, locally, for the most part, farmed the spinning, weaving and dyeing to specialist workshops in the city, then marketed the cloth opportunistically; sometimes supplying local dealers, on other occasions sending it out through Southampton for the export trade. He was becoming known in the city, at least within the cloth trade.

Charles had found his wife, Ethel, in Dorset, where she had spent the summer with her family, avoiding the dangers of Bridgewater. She had not settled in Salisbury and hated the noise, impatience and rude manners. She longed to be able to return to their old life beside the stream, where the men were tread walking the long broad lengths of cloth on her last day at the mill. She left Charles in no doubt of her intention to return to Somerset as soon as it was safe to do so.

Ethel complained frequently that she knew no one in Salisbury and Charles consoled her with the prospect of a visit as the days lengthened, though he was fearful. The military had spies everywhere and paid for information.

But Ethel was so unhappy that he could not delay it much longer. He let it be known that he was seeking new sources of wool supply and thought the chalk hills of Dorset might be worth looking at. He asked around in the trade and was given a few names and places; no one would be very surprised if he disappeared for a few weeks.

Early one morning in May, Charles and Ethel set off on the road for Southampton. The road had suffered from heavy, continuous traffic during the winter months, when fully laden oxcarts had created deep ruts and mud wallows. Some attempt had been made to improve the important road to the dock at Southampton, but this would be a constant labour throughout the year, and a losing battle after October. They stopped at a road-side inn for an hour, taking care to make it known that they were looking to purchase wool, asking innocently if there were many sheep in the area. Following advice, they turned off the

Southampton Road and travelled westwards at Fordingbridge, eventually reaching Cranborne before nightfall.

Over the next few days, they made their way towards the Blackdown Hills, making contacts for local supply of wool. These western districts were quite convenient to supply their old mill, though when they learned there was still a military presence in Bridgewater, they decided to approach from the west, avoiding the town entirely.

Their old home was desolate and in a terrible state of neglect. After a few hours, they left the mill and rode south to an inn they had visited earlier. They took a room for a couple of nights, planning to return to the mill in the morning. It was difficult to know where to start with the desolate house, but Ethel soon set about the kitchen and had a fire going within the hour. Damp and musty bedding was hung out on a clothesline till that was full, and on rose bushes and apple trees thereafter. A few passers-by stopped to chat, and around the time of the mid-day meal, a familiar face wearing a broad grin came into the yard.

"I 'eard summat was goin on. 'ow be you all?"

Charles spun around. "Albert, Albert, I am so glad you are well."

Ethel, hearing their loud voices, rushed from the house and threw her arms around Albert. "Oh, how are you? How is everyone?"

"Oh well, 'twere a bad time. A lot of young fellers were took away and haven't been seen since. An' Bridgewater were hard hit last summer, but they be getting a bit together again."

"And you, Albert... have you been well?"

He hesitated before answering,

"My girls ave been lookin atter I."

Ethel looked straight at Albert and saw his worn face. "And your wife?"

"She were bad for a few days atter Christmas, then went sudden."

"Oh, Albert. Come in and sit down, we are about ready to eat, and the fire is lit."

Albert leaned back against the wooden upright of the old settle, his head striking it firmly, causing his mug of hot water to slurp threateningly. This was his happiest day for many months.

Ethel laid her hand lightly on his shoulder.

"Steady, Albert. Don't waste it, now."

"No, missus, I won't. 'tis too good to lose."

He drew a piece of burnt crust from the mug and sucked it appreciatively. Then he turned to Charles.

"So, what do want me to get on with first?"

"Well, let's clean everything up. There's a leak in the weaving shed and I don't know what else. Can you get anyone to give you a hand?"

"Oh, no doubt I can. Are you staying long?"

Charles hesitated. "I have to return to Salisbury in a few days."

Ethel said nothing, but her face was frozen.

Late in the day, the sun getting low, Charles and Ethel set off for their lodgings at the inn. Ethel called out, "God be with you, Albert!"

He replied, "I'll see if I can get someone to give me a hand tomorrow."

They moved off down the road, the pony a bit frisky after a long idle day. Charles, concentrating hard, was gloomy.

"I suppose we'll get it back together in time, but I'll have to bring some more cash with me, when I come back. But it is a long ride to Salisbury. Do you think you can get the house fit to live in again?"

Ethel nodded her head. "Perhaps Albert can find me a girl to help in the house, and live in."

For three days they all worked hard, though Ethel and Charles arrived late one morning, having purchased a second pony and trap from a man they met at the inn. They had taken the little horse for a trial run, and she seemed to be a nice, quiet pony. As soon as the deal was settled, Ethel jumped back into the trap and set off for the mill, with Charles following behind. They had all their belongings with them, and that night they slept in their own house again.

Albert brought a girl, his niece, and it was arranged that she would sleep in the house, too. Charles felt he could safely leave Ethel with Albert and his niece, and prepared to leave early the following day, after a long discussion with Albert. They were both concerned about the weaving loom, which someone had damaged, probably while trying to steal mechanical parts from it. Albert thought he knew someone who could repair it but finding a suitable weaver would be more difficult; the young man they had once employed was among the missing, but whether dead, captured, or he had simply left the area, no one knew.

Before dawn, Charles set off alone, taking the direct route through Bridgewater. The town was relatively quiet, only a few people were opening up their shops as he passed through, but still he left the town with a sense of relief. In any event, he could hardly stop, for he must reach Bath before dark.

CHAPTER THREE

Poor Widow.

The folk tale of the poor widow who lived in her cottage with her two daughters and an amazing cockerel was often told, but not till Chaucer's *The Canterbury Tales* was published a few years hence would it be carried down the centuries.

A poor widwe, somdel stape (somewhat advanced) in age,
Was whilom dwelling in a narwe (narrow)cottage,
Bisyde a grove, standing in a dale.
This widwe, of which I tell you my tale,
Sin thilke day that she was last a wyf,
In pacience ladde (led) a ful simple lyf,
For litel was hir catel and hir rente;
By housbondrye, of such as God hir sente,
She found (kept?) hir-self and eek (also) hir doghtren (daughters) two.
Three large sowes had she, and nomo,
Three kyne (cows), and eek (also) a sheep that highte (was called) Malle,

Full sooty was her bour, and eek (also) her halle,
In which she eet ful many a sclender meel,
Of poynaunt (piquant) sauce hir needed never a deel,
No dayntee morsel passed thurgh hir throte;
Her dyete was accordant to hir cote.

Beyond the seaport of Bridgewater, another such widow lived with her two daughters in just such a narrow cottage of two rooms, with a little land surrounding. Her few animals and fowls sustained her family; a reduced family since the dreadful day her husband and son had been hacked down in revenge for the Peasants' Revolt.

Weeks and months had passed slowly since, but the changing seasons had healed her heart a little. Her cows gazed at her with uncomprehending eyes, passively grateful when she removed their milk and eased the discomfort of their heavy udders. A daily routine of feeding and caring for her little herds and flocks gave purpose to her life, but essential cheese-making, and the vegetable garden, left little time to clean the house or her own clothes.

In the first summer of her widowhood, the fragrance of mown grass wilting under a hot sun had lifted her spirits for a few days and brought an unaccustomed spring to her step. Helped by her brother and neighbours, she had been able to manage the exhausting work, making enough hay to get her cows through the winter. Heavy labour and human companionship proved an effective therapy for an aching heart.

The ricks of hay were a comforting sight throughout the next winter, though they diminished with worrying speed before the grass grew again. In March, an intensely bright sun behind leafless trees in a cold blue sky exposed the dust and grime of her neglected cottage. The widow could no longer ignore the layers of dust in unforgiving sunlight.

The daughters were press ganged into cleaning duties, though neither they nor their mother were rightly sure where to start.

By the end of the day, the sheepskin bedding and clothes had been hung on the bushes and beaten thoroughly. The small amount of furniture had been removed and the floors swept clean. Fresh new straw had been lightly stuffed into woven sacks.

As the day passed, the cows reminded the widow of milking time. Leaving the girls to carry everything back into the house, the widow collected her bucket and stool and a bit of food for the first cow. It was a relief to sit down with her face against Bluebell's friendly flank and to stroke her warm udder.

Spring and summer passed in a disorderly progression of cows calving, months of milking, and cheese-making leading on to regular visits by a succession of cheese buyers; hard and anxious men, for the most part, but one sympathetic to her situation offered a slightly better price and sometimes joined her for a meal. She came to enjoy his company and looked forward to his return.

Life continued its seasonal course; the girls grew older and stronger and better able to help their mother. Emma, the eldest was now twelve years old, the youngest a couple of years less, and they would wander off around the village with their friends and cousins.

One day, the cheese buyer arrived with a strikingly attractive young assistant. Emma was mesmerised and could not take her eyes off him, and he responded to her intense interest.

Though only six weeks later, it seemed an age till the cheese buyer and his assistant came again. The young couple went off together to bring the cows in for milking, and the assistant cheese buyer even took a stool and bucket to milk one of the cows himself. Between them they completed the milking, leaving Mother to entertain the senior buyer.

The sympathetic cheese buyer took to stopping overnight at the house of the widow's brother, but throughout the lean winter months, there was no sign of the gorgeous assistant cheese buyer. Emma's agonies were only aggravated by her happy, giggling mother.

There came a day when the cheese buyer arrived on a Saturday, and at a time of year when there was no cheese ready for sale. On the Sunday, he returned to the widow's house and suggested he harness the horses and get ready to drive the family into Bridgewater.

They passed across the Parrett with tide rushing in, swiftly covering the mud banks to create a broad sheet of water, the girls slightly overawed by this demonstration of energy and power. By the time they reached the harbour, it was almost high tide, and the crew of a small freighter moored to the harbour wall were making busy clearing the deck and lashing down.

"Where are you heading for?" asked the cheese buyer of a young deckhand.

"We be bound for Bristol."

"What are you taking up to Bristol, then?"

"Oh, bales of cloth, mostly."

"How long will that take?"

"Oh, it'll be slow, I reckon, till we get a good westerly. We won't get far fighting the tide out there without wind."

The skipper came up from below.

"Hoi, hoi, don't stand about talking. We have to get downriver on the falling tide, you know."

The crewman made himself busy, and in a few minutes the mooring ropes were cast off, though the freighter hardly moved. Imperceptibly she crept towards the harbour gates as a very weak flow of water bore her towards the river. Emma could not help but notice the crewman's deep suntan, nor the wonderful muscles of his upper arms. How tightly would he hold her, she wondered?

For another hour they could see the single mast above the sand dunes as the boat made slow but accelerating progress along the narrow, twisting river. The skipper would hope to be carried out into the Bristol Channel beyond the mud flats of Bridgewater Bay where he could wait for the rising tide; a force of water that would carry him swiftly towards Bristol for several hours, even without a helpful wind.

As the boat disappeared, the girls wandered away from the harbour wall. Their mother turned to watch them, urging caution. She leaned back and found a supporting arm around her shoulders. She smiled shyly. He did not remove his arm. This was a comfort she had forgotten during the hard and lonely years.

At length they stirred themselves and began to wonder where they might find the girls. The girls, meanwhile, had found a group of boys who were practising hand to hand combat; a form of wrestling with no holds barred. The winner would be challenged by one bystander after another until eventually beaten by physical exhaustion. The most cunning boys would hang back till the strongest had been eliminated. A couple of older men encouraged the contest while assessing the boy's potential for more advanced military skills.

The boys who had been eliminated and had lost interest in the contest chatted to the girls, who were suitably impressed by the display of virility and valour. The eldest daughter was quickly coming to the conclusion that the port of Bridgewater was far more exciting than life in the countryside.

Within a few weeks, the cheese factor had arranged for Emma to start work at the house of a business contact. She would return to her mother on Sundays, ostensibly to attend church with the family, but she had outgrown the patient life on the farm and preferred to frequent the port during her time off.

Emma was working at the house of a comfortably wealthy young family, as a cleaner and kitchen assistant. The first few days were quite strange, and she was slightly overawed by the obvious wealth of the family. She was also astonished to discover how much effort went into keeping the house clean each day of the week; she even had to carry out a light dusting on Sunday before her few hours off duty. But she came to enjoy the cleanliness and soon thought it to be normal.

Emma ate with the staff and ate well. After dinner had been served and cleared away, the leftovers were re-heated and what was left of the big joint of meat was carved and shared around by the cook.

There were four people working in the house, under the direction of the cook/housekeeper. The young wife had two small children and was pregnant again.

Emma was quite untrained for domestic service, and it was immediately apparent she was best suited for the care of the two children; her knowledge of food preparation and cooking were completely inadequate. She worked hard, however, and was keen to learn. The young mother began to trust her with the children and, over many months, came to depend on the calm and sensible village girl.

But Emma lived for her day off. After the essential dusting, she joined the short family procession to church. She walked behind her mistress, ready to assist with the two children. Emma was becoming attached to the little girls and enjoyed the parade through the town.

The understanding was that on each Sunday she would return to her mother's house, attending the evening service with her family, before returning to her employer in Bridgewater before nightfall. And for a few weeks, this she diligently did. But as she came to know people of her own age, she spent more and more time in the town, and family visits became shorter and shorter. Her mother seemed to be quite engrossed with the sympathetic cheese buyer, and scarcely noticed.

One Sunday, the same freighter Emma had seen a few months earlier was tied to the harbour wall again. Though she walked up and down several times, and quite slowly, she saw no one on the boat. She spoke to an acquaintance recently made, asking if he recognised the freighter. He looked at it without much interest and muttered that he thought he had seen it before. Emma wondered where the crew might be and wandered along the short streets near the harbour, returning to the boat at intervals. She could not wait much longer, for a late return from her half day would be questioned.

Sadly, reluctantly, she had turned away, when almost immediately she saw three young men coming towards her. Emma's heart skipped a beat when she saw the deckhand with the rather fine biceps. Something in the expression on her face encouraged him to pause, though his shipmates did not.

Emma spoke first. "How often do you come into Bridgewater?"

"Whenever we have an order."

"Well, how often is that?"

"Oh, I don't know… four weeks, maybe six, I suppose."

"I can only get out on a Sunday after church."

"Where do you work?"

"Well, I am going there now. Do you want to see the way?"

But it would be four months before the boat came in again on a Sunday. The family were walking to church and Emma was concentrating on the little children when she heard a low whistle. She looked up, and her delighted smile told him all he needed to know.

He was still there when she came out of church, and later again, when she had returned to the big house and changed out of her Sunday best for her precious afternoon off.

CHAPTER FOUR

Cedric's Tale.

Cedric, an innocent boy from White Clyffe swept up in the excitement and righteous anger of the Peasants' Revolt, had found himself twice imprisoned since 1381; press ganged to serve in a ship controlled by Richard II, now captured by the French and held in a military guard room. There were long, empty days, sometimes spent reflecting on the bright, cheerful young man who had seen no danger in campaigning for greater freedom, and longer nights, wondering if he would ever see his family again.

He and his fellow captives were put to work maintaining the grounds and buildings. They were all young and inexperienced sailors and posed no threat to the French military forces. Over the next few months, they picked up a smattering of conversational French, which allowed a sensible working relationship to develop. Having gained the trust of his captors, Cedric had been put on gardening duties in the governor's garden sometimes with others, but increasingly alone. The governor's wife had been sympathetic, and when working alone, he had occasionally been invited to have his lunch in the house on a wet day. But these were secretive visits controlled by a lonely, childless wife.

One day, an English freighter pulled into port with a load of English cloth. Some of the prisoners were detailed to unload the cloth, but Cedric was still on gardening duty.

The next day, he followed the routine of many weeks. After taking instructions from the governor's wife, he concentrated on the work in hand. In fact, he thoroughly enjoyed it, and took great pride in the appearance of the garden. Leaving the garden at the usual time, he entered a small area of woodland that formed part of the governor's grounds. He went to a thicket of thorn where he had previously hidden a rough outer garment lent to him one wet day by the kindly governor's wife. He did not move again until it was quite dark.

Walking away from the barracks and the port, Cedric moved upriver for more than an hour, till he found an up-turned fisherman's boat. He stood quietly and looked around, but could see no one, so he righted the boat and slid it into the water, then rowed downriver, searching among the boats near the river mouth. As time passed, he began to wonder if the English boat had already set sail, and thought he would stowaway on any large boat, wherever it was going.

The sky was lightening, and he worried that he would have to move soon, to be safe. Then he saw her. He tied his rowing boat to another large boat and slipped into the water, swimming to the English freighter.

He waited in the water between the boat and the bank. Almost at once he heard voices; they were coming closer, and the speakers were clearly the worse for drink. They were crewmen, making the most of their last night in port. After they had gone below, he washed his feet and followed up the gangplank, quickly hiding in the sail locker, burrowing down deep, out of view.

The boat moved on the next tide, and the motion was unmistakeable, even lying in the dark, low down in the sail locker. He wondered how the drunken crew were coping after only a few hours of sleep. He must find something to eat and drink before long, but he knew he must stay out of sight till after dark, when the boat was well away from the French shore.

After what seemed like hours, he heard voices above, and it was a comfort to hear English spoken again. But he must wait till all was quiet.

When he could wait no longer, Cedric stealthily moved the sail cloths away, lifted the lid very slowly, and looked around the deck, which appeared to be deserted. So, as quietly as he could, he came out of the locker and moved to the side of the boat. And then he heard footsteps. He turned, looked out to sea, opened the front of his trousers, and relieved himself over the side.

"Better out than in, I daresay. Thee better get below before you are caught up here."

Cedric nodded and moved along the ship,

"No, no, don't go that way. Are you still drunk?"

Cedric admitted he was and stumbled quite convincingly in the other direction, found the steps, and went below. He must find water at any cost. He saw some bread and, however hard and stale, it was a feast. Behind him a door opened, and by the light of a candle, he was seen.

"Who be you, then?"

"Oh, I come on board to help with the cloth."

"Well, it's all unloaded and left in France. Have you been to sea before? You sound like a country boy to me."

"Yeah, well I am. Or I was, till I was press ganged."

"You didn't escape from the military, did you?"

"No. We ran aground on the French coast. They attacked us, took us young 'uns away, and killed all the others."

"Boys, we got a stowaway. Better go to the skipper."

A few hours later, the ship docked and lay still in an unknown harbour. Cedric was locked up in a cell without light, but at least he was supplied with bread and water. For the third time, he was a prisoner; he reflected again on the cheerful optimistic young man from White Clyffe, who saw no danger to himself, nor malice in others.

A few days later, he is scrubbing the deck with two other deckhands. Neither of them knew where they were bound, though all recognised that the ship was now heading south. The deckhands had loaded wool at Southampton, and Cedric was not released till they were well out in the English Channel. But now the wind was getting up and lifting the flat-bottomed boat like a toy. Cedric had not found his sea legs and was soon leaning over the side of the boat. His naval career had only lasted a few months, and he had spent more time in a French guardroom on dry land. During the miseries of seasickness, he thought fondly of the governor's wife, and almost wished he were still there.

During the second night, the winds eased, and the storm was followed by quieter weather and flatter seas. Then, one morning, they saw land on the port bow, and soon there were more birds searching the boat for food. Scrubbing duties were supervised more closely as the seagulls soiled the deck relentlessly. After a few hours, they passed close enough to see people on the shore of a jagged rock, which slipped astern as gently as it had appeared and was gone from sight again.

The next morning, they were heading into a clear sunrise with a following westerly breeze. For several days, they made slow progress in calm seas and warm sunshine. Even the first mate seemed to relax, though the skipper hardly appeared on the open deck. He was, however, issuing orders to check the cargo below decks, consisting of large bales of wool. Cedric surmised that he was preparing to deal with the wool buyers at the next port. The mate picked up from the ship's gossip that

Cedric had worked in the wool trade, though none knew how short his career had been.

They passed a succession of islands. Long, low-sided rowing galleys, sometimes with a sail to catch a favourable wind, travelled the short journeys from port to port at quite high speeds. The more knowing among the crew reckoned they would not last long in an Atlantic storm and guessed they would stay in port if it got choppy.

Two days later, the ship nosed into a foreign port. Cedric had joined the group, inspecting the wool, and his ability to read and write had been noticed. At first light, samples of wool were selected and displayed on the dock beside the moored boat, under the control of the skipper.

Cedric compared the samples.

"They all right, boy?" It was a voice he did not recognise, it was the gruff old skipper.

Cedric spun around quickly, came to attention and said,

"Yes, sir, they are a very even selection."

"Well, let's see how we sell them. Do you speak Italian, boy?"

"No, sir, but I got a bit of French."

"Well, I want a record of our sales, but we'll do that in English."

Cedric and the mate remained with the dockside display throughout the morning, but certain people were taken on the boat to inspect the wool in the hold. A difficult conversation in broken English and fractured Italian somehow reached a conclusion, and deals were struck. Later in the day, horses and wagons appeared on the dock, and the boat moved along to a simple hoist. The big bales were then lifted from the hold and loaded onto the wagons. By the end of the day, two principal buyers had removed their purchases, and smaller orders were dealt with the next morning.

People passed along the wharf throughout the day, just sightseeing, apparently. Hot food vendors set up beside the main pathways, and other traders brought things for sale; fishermen tied up near the steps leading down to a small boat jetty. In no time, a small market had set up spontaneously. Cedric was astonished by the beautiful girls with liquid brown eyes and long hair, which they tossed with a little flick of the head. They would smile briefly, turn away, and hardly ever look back to see the effect.

On the second day, the wool was sold slowly and with difficulty at the lock-side. Everyone seemed to hang back reluctantly, till the skipper clapped his hands and reduced his prices. And then the rush started as the townspeople began to fear the wool would all be gone before they could secure some for themselves.

"Now then, boy, stop eyeing up those girls and get to work. I need some money to provide food for the journey home."

When the skipper was out of earshot, the mate said,

"This is where he makes money for 'imself. All those big orders were sold by the brokers before we left Southampton."

The following morning, the skipper was nowhere to be seen. The mate had the crew cleaning the boat, and some unsold wool was offered for sale at the dockside, but there were few people and little enthusiasm.

Around mid-day, a procession of carts protected by armed guards came into the docks and pulled up beside Jolecia. The skipper and the Genoese traders supervised the transfer of an evidently valued cargo into the hold of the ship. Records were signed by all parties and the skipper took his record straight to his cabin before returning to the dockside. Further discussion for an hour, apparently successful, then a smaller quantity was taken from the carts and placed on the dockside. The skipper gave a signal, and the mate took some crew men to collect these mysterious packages, which were transferred straight to the skipper's cabin.

Cedric glanced at the mate, with a raised eyebrow.

"Spices. That is why we've come all the way to Genoa; this small load of spices is probably worth more than the full load of wool we brought over. And somewhere, on the way back, we'll probably fill the rest of the hold with wine."

The return journey across the Mediterranean was slower in the face of the same westerly that had brought them to Genoa so helpfully.

At length, they tacked and crabbed through Gibraltar and out into the Atlantic. The mountainous seas soon had Cedric heaving over the side of the boat again, to the amusement of most of the crew.

Fortunately, it was a relatively short journey to the next port, on the Tagus River. Calm water again, a narrow entrance at first, which then widened out into a large, natural harbour. Despite a recent history of earthquakes, the town had retained some Moorish architecture, having only been re-conquered by Christian forces two centuries earlier, but the skipper had little interest in the scenery. As the mate had forecast, he intended to fill the hold with cheap Portuguese wine for the London trade.

Only one night was spent in Lisbon, to Cedric's disappointment, but the prospect of returning to England led him to hope he might make contact with his family somehow. The skipper had been anxious not to linger once he learned that Lisbon was sliding into civil war, though he greatly admired their boats when he saw them in Lisbon harbour. The Portuguese were Atlantic sailors, developing their trade with North African countries, and were pioneer developers of truly seaworthy Atlantic sailing ships.

Then several days spent in the Atlantic, with Cedric gradually acclimatising to the pitching and heaving of the lumpy flat-bottomed boat, before turning into the English Channel, which was not noticeably calmer. Through the straights and, for Cedric, there was a first view of the White Cliffs of Dover, something which usually generates the warmth of homecoming for experienced English sailors. A leisurely cruise up the Thames on an in-coming tide before a few hours at anchor, waiting for the next tide, provided a pleasant change from the open seas.

The moment they landed, the skipper was off to meet the brokers, and the mate was in charge of the ship. Two hours of cleaning and polishing left the boat looking quite presentable, but they all knew everything would explode into chaos when the skipper returned.

The wine came off first, and the brokers were able to move this out to retailers quite quickly. The spices the skipper had bought on behalf of the brokers were a complex cargo, and of high value. It was late in the day before the deals were completed to all round satisfaction.

The skipper came aboard again in good humour and announced, "We'll unload the rest of it first thing tomorrow, then move to the wool wharf on the last of the tide. And tomorrow night, I'll take you to the stews."

This was taken in good spirit and rough humour by the crew, though Cedric did not fully grasp the significance at first.

After they had eaten, some of the crew wandered off into town, but they would not be paid till the holds were emptied tomorrow, so could only watch the crowds.

It was a balmy evening in London, and Cedric sat on the lid of the sail locker till the skipper came towards him, when he stood up smartly.

"No, I'll join you there. It's a nice evening. And good to be back in England again."

Cedric nodded. "There have been many times when I thought I'd never see England again, this last two years."

"I know you came as a stowaway, but I'll pay you tomorrow, with all the others. You are a bright lad, and if you stay with me, I'll train you up. You look as though you might have a good head for business."

Cedric took time to reflect before he replied, and the skipper waited.

"I need to get a message to my family. They don't know if I'm alive or dead and must be very worried."

"We'll be back in Southampton before long, and if you sign up with me, I'll let you have time off to go back to Wiltshire. But we've got a few short trips to do first, taking wool to Calais."

"That's fine then. I'll do it. I'll sign up with you."

"Good; tomorrow night we'll celebrate. You know where we are going?"

"Yeah, the boys told me."

"We'll find someone young and clean. That'll be alright."

They sat together for some minutes without speaking, then without warning, the skipper turned to Cedric and said, "You were held by the French, I've heard?"

Cedric paused to collect his thoughts. "We ran aground in a storm and were up on a mud bank. The armed men left us and hid up in the rocks, before the French reached us. Our soldiers always did a lot of shouting, but they just disappeared. We were taken away and held in the barracks a few miles away."

"What boat were you on?"

"Jezebel."

"Oh, I knew 'er. She were commandeered like a good many others' in Southampton. I don't bide there a minute longer than I 'ave to. Southampton is dangerous fer that."

Cedric noticed that he slipped into West Country dialect at times and asked, "Do you come from Southampton?"

"Nearby. My uncles had a farm in Hampshire, but that were long ago."

Next morning, bright and early, as planned, the spices were unloaded and taken away by the brokers. The skipper went ashore to the brokers' offices again to collect his money, leaving most of it on account. It was not safe to wander around London carrying a lot of money, as anyone knew. But he kept his own written record, signed and sealed by the broker, and that was good in most English ports, and even a few foreign places.

The wool wharf was situated between the Tower and London Bridge and was a source of great wealth for a few influential people in the city. In addition, the tax on wool exports collected on this wharf, and a number of small provincial wharves, provided one third of the entire income of the king. His military conflicts with France and Scotland were entirely dependent on this trade.

The leading figures in the trade were often lord mayors of London or, if not, they hoped to become so. The richest among them even provided large loans to the king to ease temporary embarrassments and were widely thought to be among the king's most important supporters.

Not far from the wool wharf was a quay devoted to prostitution known as 'the stews', and this is where the skipper took his crew for a jolly evening out after paying them for the long trip to Genoa and return. The owner of the establishment clearly knew the skipper as an old friend and she, in return for him bringing his robust, healthy and vigorous young men, rewarded the skipper personally.

As the drink flowed, voices rose with increasing confidence, and one by one the lubricated young men succumbed to temptation. Cedric was reserved by nature, and quietly spoken. He was not accustomed to strong drink, but knew he must buy his own round, which he did quite early in the evening. He drank extremely slowly and was still in control of his feelings when a slightly older girl sat next to him. She was careful not to shock him, but asked about his travels, which he described with enthusiasm, having visited countries he had scarcely heard of before. She recognised his accent and surprised him by guessing that he came from Wiltshire.

"My mother came from Wiltshire," she explained, "and talked just like you."

By happy coincidence, her mother had lived in Chippenham, only three hours' walk from White Clyffe, and Cedric immediately asked her if she still had contact with anyone there, as he had to get a message to his parents.

"Come with me and you can write a note for them."

To a resounding cheer from the ship's crew, the girl led Cedric upstairs, where the only furniture was a bed. She went to Madame and returned with a quill and a small piece of imported paper. They sat next to each other as he wrote a short message, which he knew would be a comfort for his mother.

"You are a wonderful son for any mother, and this will make her happy."

Quite spontaneously, Jane leaned forward, turned her head, and kissed Cedric warmly on the mouth. Startled, his response was too slow, and only as she withdrew did he try to kiss her in response. Modestly, she laid the palm of her hand against his chest. His forward movement forced her backwards, and they found themselves lying on the bed, when at last he kissed her in response. Had her hand not stroked the back of his neck, he might well have recovered his composure, but the combination of her practised skills and his warm feelings for her kindness to him made this impossible.

"Oh, you needed that, you hungry sailor. It must have been a long and lonely time."

Weakly Cedric smiled and agreed that it had been. "Now, I owe you for the writing paper, don't forget."

The separate aspects of the transaction were completed, and she led him downstairs to the rowdy crew below.

"Are you here most nights?" he asked.

"I'll be here tomorrow," Jane replied, and squeezed his hand before turning away to talk to two new arrivals.

Next morning, most of the crew were in high spirits and re-living the supposed exploits of the night before, but the skipper was already arranging business on the busy wool wharf. All wool passing out through the wharf had to be weighed and taxed, and when the tax had been paid, the sack of wool was stamped by two different people in an attempt to prevent fraud. But powerful individuals had an interest in this trade and were always looking for ways to reduce their tax liability. There were people milling around on the wharf, hustling and bustling in all directions.

Cedric noticed an older man with long white hair, though also with surprisingly black, bushy eyebrows. He moved almost languidly, though his eyes were alert enough, and when he spoke, he had the workers' full attention. He was clearly the man in charge, and one of the two parties holding the all-important stamp that certified the payment of tax.

But soon Cedric and the entire crew were busy carrying sacks of wool into the hold. The experienced hands worked at a pace they could sustain for the whole day, though did not discourage any enthusiastic novices who might be tempted to rush. The job was completed in good time, for the skipper to think of catching the last of the falling tide. Cedric was dismayed to realise he would not be able to see the considerate girl of the night before, but this trade from London to Calais was routine work, not highly paid, and the skipper could not afford to waste time. Still, Cedric consoled himself, there might only be a few of these short journeys before their return to Southampton, with the opportunity to see his family again at White Clyffe.

The few journeys taking repeat loads to Calais became many, and it was three full months before Jolecia was brought into Southampton. Cedric was paid off and assured that he would be taken on again by the skipper. They walked together to the broker's office, and the skipper introduced him to the head of the business.

"Young Cedric here has signed up with me but needs to get to his family. He'll be back in a month, and I'll take him on again. Could you put him to work for a week or two till I return?"

The broker looked at Cedric in silence, and then nodded his head. He passed a piece of paper to Cedric, saying, "Put your name down here and the name of the ship, and we'll take it from there."

Cedric wrote the details with some confidence, and the broker remarked, "You've got a good hand."

"Our father taught us all to write when we were quite young. I need to make my way to Wiltshire. Do you know if there are any carriers heading that way who could use a hand on the journey?"

"There is regular traffic to Salisbury, but probably less going on to Warminster or Devizes. Hang about here for a while and you'll see people loading who might be glad of a hand."

Cedric turned to the skipper. "Thank you, sir. I'll be off now and see what I can find."

"We'll be here for a couple of days, so if you can't get away tonight, come back on board."

After Cedric had left them, the broker looked at the skipper and asked, "Navy?"

The skipper smiled and nodded. "The Jezebel from Southampton."

"Ah, I remember. She went down a year ago."

"The French held him, but he escaped. Sound lad."

Chapter Five

Return to White Clyffe.

The family had come into the house late in the day for the evening meal, as they always did. Morris and the two boys, Henry and Bryce, had been labouring hard in the fields, and the girls, who had worked almost as long with the cheese, now helped their mother with the main meal of the day.

The men were settling down and starting to relax, their feet feeling unusually light after plodding in clay for hours. Peronell, who was stirring the pot on the fire, let out a piercing scream that might have been in terror or disbelief, for she had seen a human form moving towards the house. She went to the door and ran and ran, screaming hysterically, with her arms outstretched.

Morris grumbled. "Whatever be the matter with that girl now?"

Reluctantly, he dragged himself to his feet. When he reached the door, he saw that she had her arms around a young man and had subsided into incoherent sobbing. Morris moved closer and saw who had arrived. "Yer everyone, 'tis our Cedric, come and zee!"

The evening passed in a haze, and they all drank too much beer, and the questions, the questions. "What happened to you? Why has it been so long? How did you get away?"

Slowly, between interruptions, Cedric told his story, and gradually they all understood why he had not been able to let them know where, or how, he was; except for his mother, who was a pale, timid figure, and only a shadow of the robust woman he remembered. She held her head in her hands, all colour drained from her face. "Do you know what you have done to me, you wicked boy?"

The room fell silent.

"Look at me. You see what you have done? You don't even know what I have suffered."

Morris sought to soothe her. "Now, Mother, don't take on so."

"I'll take on if I need to. None of ee know what I've suffered."

An awkward pause. No one quite knew what to say.

Morris cleared his throat. "Well, come on, look... we got an early start tomorrow, and you must be tired too, Cedric, after that journey?"

But Cedric was too wound up to sleep. His mind kept returning to his poor mother, who was now so frail. Had he really been the cause of her decline? But what could he have done? He had been locked up, far away, and he did get back as soon as he could. He wondered what had happened to the message he had tried to send. And he thought again of the girl who had seemed so kind and obliging. Perhaps he would see her again when he returned to the old skipper and Jolecia.

Cedric did not wake until disturbed by his brothers as they got ready to work, then slept again, more heavily than before. His sister, Peronell brought him a mug of hot water and some bread. She was so thrilled to have him home, safe and well. It quite made up for his anxious and fretful mother.

"I've just got to turn some cheese, then we can have a walk around, if you want," she told him.

"Oh, I'll give you a hand."

Cedric had forgotten so much in two years, and his younger brothers were now very confident in their work around the farm. They were taking advantage of the dry weather to work the fallow ahead of sowing the next crop of wheat. They invited him to take the plough, but he declined. It was a long time since he had left the farm to work in the wool trade in Calne.

Peronnell chattered happily and slipped her arm through his as they strolled along the village street. There seemed to be surprisingly few people about on a fine morning. Were they at work? Or hiding from someone they did not recognise? Cedric and Peronell turned into the graveyard to look at the family graves; Peronnel tidied the flowers and took away some that were dying back. They continued beyond the church to the end of the village. In truth, there was not much to look at; nothing seemed to have happened while Cedric had been up and down the English Channel and across the Mediterranean to Genoa and imprisoned by the French. He wondered how he might fill the days till it was time to return to Southampton.

After a period of silence, he said, "I might go to Calne and see the people I used to work with."

Another silence, then Peronell spoke, covering her disappointment bravely. "Oh, will you? When will you do that?"

"Oh, in a day or two, I 'spose."

"Perhaps I could come. We might need to get something from town. I'll ask father."

They turned and walked back through the village. A couple of people nodded to Peronell but neither of them spoke.

*   *   *

Cedric enjoyed the journey into Calne with his sisters on a lovely day early in September, low mist rising, the air quite still. They found a few market stalls already set up; others not quite so advanced were still being put together. A steady chatter: "Hold the other end—no, down a bit", "Come on, get the table ready, and mind those eggs, will 'ee."

Morris had agreed that both girls could accompany Cedric, and if they were going, they might as well take something to sell. A few early shoppers inspected the stalls, pausing to chat to Peronnell and other people they knew, but no one recognised Cedric.

After an hour, the crowd had thickened, and his sisters were busy with customers. Cedric waved to Peronell and made a gesture to indicate that he was going to walk around the town. He walked across the green beside the old church and made his way to the Marden. The river was low after many weeks of dry weather, and he paused to look into the clear water. He had the feeling he was being watched and was not completely surprised when someone greeted him. "Cedric, isn't it? Haven't seen you for years."

"No, I have been away at sea."

Then, looking at the speaker for the first time, he recognised a fellow apprentice from his short career in the cloth trade.

"Oh, hello. How are things going?"

"Oh, going on quite steady, I suppose. Are you staying long?"

"I have to rejoin my ship in a month, so will be around for a bit. Are you still at the mill?"

A silent nod, a shuffling diffidence in his manner, suggested uncertainty and ebbing confidence. Distracted by an acquaintance who called to him, he turned with relief to respond. When the conversation ended, Cedric said,

"I'd quite like to see the old mill again."

"Well, I'm sure that will be alright, if we are not too busy. But I must get back now."

"Look, I'll come with you. I might get lost on my own."

Too nervous to laugh, the apprentice nodded, and they walked silently to the mill.

Cedric waited outside for several minutes, till his former master appeared, looking left and right before talking.

"When you disappeared, I didn't know what to think, but I feared the worst. They came 'ere asking if we knew anyone mixed up wi' the clamour, but I did'n know nuthin. They be still about, you know. I should bide low and get back to sea, if I were you. A lot of people have died over this. But I be glad to see you be awright." And with that he turned away, went back into the mill, and secured the door behind him.

Cedric made his way back to the river below the church but did not return to the market. Instead, he walked along the bank till he was clear of the town. Quite a small river, twisting and turning in a sheltered valley, but if he noticed its tranquil beauty, it did not register in his mind.

He now understood the danger in Calne, where he was once known, and knew he should not return to the market till the girls were ready to go home.

Cedric followed the river downstream for a couple of miles, then climbed the steep side of the valley to higher farmland. Here he made his way eastwards to pick up the road to White Clyffe before turning south to walk slowly into town. On reaching the open green, he could see that the market was still quite busy, so he wandered into the church nearby and was quite glad to find a seat against the wall.

An hour later and the girls were glad to see him but were worried that he had not eaten. Cedric helped them clear up and made no attempt to talk to anyone. Peronell noticed his subdued manner but said nothing; there was little conversation on the long walk back to White Clyffe.

The next morning, he found the opportunity to talk to his father and told him of his experience at the mill. His father understood at once. "He was quite right to warn you of the danger and is a good friend to us both."

While they were eating, after work, Morris spoke to them all.

"We must keep quiet about Cedric. Word could get back to the military. The safest place for him is back to sea."

Cedric replied. "I'd like to see Aunt Edith again before I go. But I'll stay away from Calne."

His brother tried to lighten the conversation. "You'd better get started doin' some work before you get bored. We'll teach you a bit of plowing."

A few days later, Cedric and Peronell set off to walk to Edith's place, taking care to arrive at her village after dark. For security, and the reassurance of numbers late at night, both of the brothers went. Edith was delighted to see

Cedric, for she had become so involved in the events in Salisbury during the worst days of the revolt. She had not expected to see Cedric again, but now realised he had been lucky to have been press ganged into the navy.

Again, Cedric related his experiences, but to a quieter and calmer audience. The realisation of the dangers he had faced had more impact on his brothers and sisters than on the initial telling on that first euphoric evening.

Peronell asked, "What was it like, in a French prison?"

"Oh, it was not too bad, Nell, once you got used to the food. You never knew what you were eating."

Edith was calm and reflective. "It is still not safe for anyone connected with the revolt. They are still hunting for anyone involved. You are safer at sea, well away from here."

Peronell was torn. She had been elated by her brother's return, safe, and in one piece, after months and months of not knowing if he was alive or dead, and now he was about to leave them again.

Edith read her ravaged face. "It is the safest place for him, at sea. As time passes, he will be able to come home again."

Peronell nodded dumbly, unable to control her voice.

A few days later, Cedric went to Edith's home again, but this time only with Peronell in the early hours. The final parting was lengthy and painful; Edith had to complain about her bad legs and insist that Peronell bathe them this instant. A last hurried goodbye, and Cedric was gone.

After a long, long walk to Salisbury, Cedric found a carrier who needed help with loading his bullock wagon. He agreed to give a free ride to Southampton in return for Cedric's labour. While they were loading, others stopped to ask for a ride, but only an older woman and her two children were accepted; something small passed from hand to hand, and a deal was done.

The plodding cattle went at their own pace and no other. The passengers soon became accustomed to horse-drawn carts and carriages coming up behind, passing them, and quickly disappearing from view.

Around nightfall they drew into an inn, where the carrier went inside, leaving Cedric to unhitch the bullocks and water them. The mother and children stretched their legs before climbing back onto the wagon with a mouthful of bread and a drop of water each and settling down to sleep on the wool sacks.

Cedric had a little money and went into the inn after securing the bullocks. The carrier nodded to him as he came in, talking with difficulty through a full mouth.

"The team all right?"

"Yea, they are hitched up to the wagon again."

"Well don't leave 'em too long." A subtle indication that the carrier planned to spend an extended evening in the warm and noisy bar.

Cedric was asleep and did not hear the carrier's return. He only woke to hear him cursing his reluctant cattle to lean into the harness.

Despite starting at the crack of dawn, they did not reach Southampton till mid-afternoon. The tang of the sea was unmistakeable, and the clear, fresh air was a delight. Much as he wanted to see his family again, Cedric understood that he no longer belonged on the farm.

Early next morning, he presented himself at the broker's office and asked if there was any news of Jolecia. The clerk hustled away to the back office for a few minutes, then returned to lead Cedric to the broker.

"I don't want the whole world to know our arrangements, and I suggest you keep things to yourself."

Cedric nodded in silent reply.

"I reckon she'll be a week or so. You have arrived sooner than I expected, but I can give you work for bed and board."

Cedric understood that this could be a good contact for future deals, and he should not hold out for a cash payment.

Chapter Six

Village Funeral.

Edith's sons have travelled to Salisbury to bring her back to her old home. She has spent another winter with Harry, the friendly, talkative man, and now, as the celandines and bluebells come into flower, she has died. They had to ask strangers for directions but had found Harry outside his house. He talks to them in the street and shares their sorrow, then stiffens. "Do not look around, just keep talking to me." The brothers talk to each other, then to Harry again, then one removes his hat and scratches his head. He inspects the inside of his hat, as if searching for a potential flea. After whacking the hat against a post, it is replaced on his head.

"Ah, he's gone on by. You don't want to see 'ee, nor 'ee you. 'Ee be dangerous, and Edith knew about 'ee when your cousin disappeared. Don't tell 'ee nuthin."

"Did 'ee have summat to do with our Cedric, then?"

"No one knows, but some money changed hands, I daresay. Look... if you come back in the morning, Edith will be ready for 'ee."

The brothers walked back to the yard at the edge of town, where they had left the wagon and horses. "We'll load the wagon before we go back for Mother. She wouldn't want us to come all this way and go back emptyhanded, now, would she?"

*   *   *

Edith's funeral was attended by her nephews and nieces, who had walked from White Clyffe to Compton, where Edith had been married and her sons still lived. Morris, with his wife and elderly sister, Juliana, travelled by dog cart and pony.

As they approached, they saw an impressive stone building set on rising ground. The simple Norman church, built by ancient owners, had later been extended by aisles on the north and south sides. Rough Norman stonework had once been covered with white plaster, decorated with biblical scenes. These told the stories they had only heard from the priest, when no villager read the Latin bible, and even written English was an impenetrable barrier for most. Only remnants of the wall paintings remained. More recently, powerful owners had built a new chancel arch with a stairway, creating a rather fine church. Most of the family were overwhelmed by the grandeur, though later proud that Edith had received such an impressive funeral.

Morris and the family from White Clyffe, met Edith's sons and their families at the church door. Edith had been the eldest of a family of six, though of these, only Morris and herself had children; a brother and a sister had died of the plague, while another brother, un-married, had been cared for by his sister, Juliana, who stood in the church now. All Edith's living relatives attended the funeral, save for Cedric, who was busy at sea, not even aware that Edith had died.

Though she had lived so long and outlived a lifetime of friendships, the church was comfortably full; recent business contacts from the nearby market towns came to pay their respects and to strengthen friendships with the younger members of the family. They stood shoulder to shoulder in the little parish church, alongside half the populations of White Clyffe and Compton.

Since his own death, Edith's father, John, had entered the stuff of legend; already in living memory, he was the founding father of the Johnson dynasty. He had served the church as lay preacher; he had led the small group whom, for a year and a half, had collected eighty infected bodies and taken them away from their homes to a rapid burial. None knew when they might become infected, if they ever permitted themselves to dwell on the possibility.

Edith herself had lived to a great age. Born in famine, her tiny, stunted body carried the evidence of childhood starvation. On the early death of her husband, she had developed her business as a market trader, and then, as her sons grew into the place of their father, they had expanded their trade to include the neighbouring towns of Calne, Chippenham and Devizes. Edith had lived through plague, disaster, and recovery, to see a new dynamic age driven by an industry arising from the cloth trade of Salisbury; now threatened, it seemed, by riot and repression.

After the emotion of the church service and the burial, the offers of comfort and kindness to the nearest and dearest opened a flood of rising spirits. Arm in arm, they walked a few hundred yards to the family home, where a feast had been prepared. The boys had broken open a few bottles of unsold wine, though in truth, it was somewhat variable in quality;

most men turned back to honest ale that anyone could trust.

As darkness fell, a huge pile of branches and small trees was gradually fed into a thriving fire, and a fat pig was slowly roasted. Some of the fat dripped into the embers below, feeding great flames. Newly baked bread was dipped into the running fat, just to test the pork; you know, just to see how she was coming along.

Later, family and friends reminisced long into the night, reflecting on their good fortune in surviving the famine and plague to reach a point where there was an abundance of food and sufficient land for a family to feel secure. By now, the hard stuff had been circulating long enough to encourage some rough and noisy singing, though there were some merciful periods of silence. Occasionally, some young and talented voices were heard, only to be drowned out after a few minutes by loud and repeated choruses.

But underlying the abandoned, carefree and frankly drunken celebrations, they were still anxious about taxation and ambitious, war-hungry young kings. One good thing, they all agreed, was that with all the bloodshed and destruction, no one had dared bring in another poll tax since the revolt.

One by one, they dropped off to sleep; only the obsessive gloomsters continued to feed their festering minds with seditious talk.

Sometime after daybreak, people rose and stumbled out into fresh air and sunlight.

Morris was concerned that there was no one at home to milk the cows.

"Alright, Father, we'll get home now. You older ones take your time here."

The air was crisp and might have been close to a frost overnight. A ring of unburnt sticks around the fire was kicked and scuffed into a heap of hot ashes in the middle. A thin spiral of smoke rose tentatively. Soon a flicker of flame, fed by small twigs, then larger sticks, became quite a respectable fire. Someone hacked a slice of pork from the remains of the pig and spiked it on the end of his knife, then held it as close to the flames as he could bear. Stale bread was brought and toasted, and more people cut their own slices of pork. Amazingly, not all the ale from the night before had been used up. There came supplies of new bread, hot from the oven, and all vanished within minutes.

"Alright, alright, there'll be more on the way."

Late risers joined the big fire and, before long, the milkers returned from their distant farms.

A short distance away, a younger boy was trying to hit a ball with a piece of wood and, with practice, became more skilful, striking the ball higher and further. When someone caught the ball, he had to give his piece of wood to the catcher. Other boys took turns to lob the ball gently to the batter, and in turn, they all passed the piece of wood to the catcher, till the first boy came around again. He soon learned how to place the ball where no one could catch it. He was so skilful and kept the piece of wood so long that the other boys became bored and wandered away.

"Come and have something to eat, you boys, then we'll have some running races after that."

A new barrel of ale replaced the old, and the drinking resumed, though at a less frantic pace than the night before. Increasingly stupefied, the men chatted easily, almost without a care, till someone remembered the running races.

"I remember a lad from Calne wi' very long legs. 'Ee were main quick."

"There were another wi' longer legs than 'ee, but they kept getting tangled up together."

"I ain't built fer runnin'. Weight liftin' be best fer I. Now we better see how these young lads can run."

The old men looked around; impaired vision blurred further by alcohol.

"Where be they boys?"

"Well, you shouldn't have told them about running races. They be long gone. Bird nestin', I daresay."

Chapter Seven

Recovery at Bridgewater.

It was two full months before Charles returned to his old mill beyond Bridgewater, and his wife was understandably cool at his late arrival. Fortunately, he had sent a rider with cash to ensure that the repairs continued, and the pantry could be restocked.

"Well, I don't know what I can give you to eat, I've had no warning."

Charles was not too perturbed by this protest, for he could see that Ethel was already cooking for Albert and his niece, but he let it pass without comment.

"I've not been able to get away sooner. It's been difficult to find wool at a reasonable price this year, so I've been to wool sales all over, and I've had to be in Southampton a couple of times after a mess-up with the shipping broker." This was met with a long silence.

"I see you have found time to buy some books again."

"Yes, yes, I found them in Salisbury. I thought it would be nice to read to you again."

At this point the door opened, and Albert's smiling face appeared slowly in the opening.

"You made it alright, then," he said, half in question, half in comment.

"Good to be back here, Albert. How's it all going?"

"Well, I be glad you got 'ere, I need to show you one or two jobs I can't finish."

Ethel somewhat tetchily, observed "I hope you are not going out now, Charles, I'm nearly ready to serve."

"No, no, of course not."

During the meal, Albert explained that he had repaired the roofs and made the doors and shutters safe again.

"Must have been a fair few people looking about here while 't'were empty, I'd say."

"Have you got anywhere with the loom?" asked Charles.

"Well, I got a blacksmith to look at it. He'll come again and fix it, if you want him to."

"Yea, we need to get going again. I've got some wool on the way from Dorset, and we'll get that out to the spinners. Do you know how many of our old spinners will be ready to get going again?"

"I've spoke to a few. How long before we get the wool?"

"Probably about a week, I suppose."

"I'll speak to them again and see who is ready to start."

After a good meal and a hot drink in front of the fire, eyelids began to droop.

Ethel now quite anxious, warned "You two ought to get to bed before you fall on the floor. Albert has been sleeping here for a few weeks. It didn't feel safe on our own."

"Oh, thank you, Albert. It's a comfort to know you are here," said Charles.

Albert opened his eyes, "I'll go back to my place tomorrow."

Charles replied quickly, "I'll be here for a week or two to get things moving, then I'll have to get back to Salisbury. So, I hope you'll be able to keep an eye on everything here."

"Well, my old place is a cold empty house. If you want me, missus, I'll be back whenever you say."

In the morning it was raining heavily, so they spent an hour in the sheds looking for leaks and damp patches. Charles admired some new thatching and asked Albert who had he found to do it.

"Oh, I did it me self. I've thatched a main few ricks in me time. But yer look at this wool, left here for I don't know how long."

Charles shook his head in disbelief. "God, what a mess. We'll have to go through it all and clean it up as best we can. Better find a couple of people to help you, and I'll see if anyone knows of a weaver. We must get that old loom going again. And we better look at the leet when it stops raining… and I 'spose the water wheel might want a bit of work after all this time."

The day passed quickly, and Ethel looked out to see how they were getting on.

"Albert, will you eat with us again tonight?"

Charles broke in, "'Tis too late for you to think of going back to your house tonight. You better stay here."

Albert nodded happily and indicated that he was more than willing to agree.

The next day, Albert left early to hire a couple of men and took the opportunity to check that his house was still safe and in good repair. He returned just in time for the mid-day meal, which he never missed. The men he had hired would start the next day, and Albert would spend the afternoon getting a few things ready for them so that they could start as soon as they arrived. "Don't want them hanging about when they get here."

There was no further mention of him returning to his own house.

After lunch, Charles pointed out that the water wheel needed some repair, and that he thought the hatch should be raised to flush away the accumulated silt. "It won't be easy to move that hatch. It'll need a lot of raking to get rid of all that muck and weeds, I daresay."

The men arrived at sunrise the next day, and Albert had everything ready for them.

An hour later, Charles had saddled up and was ready to visit some of his business contacts. Ethel was watching Albert and the men struggling with the hatch when he called out that he was leaving, but she did not break off her conversation to say goodbye. Charles spoke quietly to his horse and moved away.

After an hour's good gallop, he allowed his horse to walk the last mile.

Charles slowly approached the cloth mill of his old friend, Frank, reflecting that they had not seen each other since those uncertain weeks before the revolt. The greetings were warm, tinged with concern for each other's experiences over the past year or so.

Charles turned back to his old mare. "I'll just give her a rub before she takes a chill."

"No, we'll look after her for you sir," said the groom.

"Thank you. I'll see you before I go."

Knowing that Bridgewater had suffered violence and murders, Charles was keen to learn how his friend had fared.

"Well, the younger fellers got mixed up with all the excitement and did not come back to work for a few weeks. Some never came back at all; a lot of people have died or been taken away, and probably will never be seen again. The older men carried on, though some of them went back to their families well away from here till it got quieter."

"So how did you manage?"

"Well, we shut down. Trade just died, and there was no sale for cloth for many months, even if we could have worked."

"Did you have any damage to the mill?"

"No, we were far enough out of town, but there was more trouble in Bridgewater itself. But how did you manage? I heard your mill was left empty for more than a year."

"I was already living in Salisbury when the revolt began. Meetings were held in towns and villages and people moved on from village to village and one town after another, till they congregated in Salisbury. And that frightened the military. They cracked down hard, arresting anyone they thought might be active and dangerous. Quite a few were executed to make room for more arrests."

"But who ran the mill down here?"

"Oh, Albert and my wife, Ethel, kept it going till things became violent. Then Ethel went to stay with her family in Dorset. I had to be very careful I was not linked with Bridgewater; there were spies and informers everywhere, and still are, even now. I did not see Ethel for a long time."

"Was the violence bad in Salisbury? I heard Bridgewater was the worst place in the south of England."

"Well yes, I think it was. Salisbury was just speeches and shouting. And it soon subsided; most people are interested in making money, in Salisbury. Though the military have a large base there and they pay for information still. Do you hear of anyone speaking of our meetings with the stewards?"

"No, nothing."

"Well, we must continue to be careful. Any suspicion of us working as a group and seeking to organise change for the better could set them worrying. And they know the villagers did not organise the rebellion alone."

"I suppose that's right."

"But I've probably taken too much of your time. There is one thing I need, and that is a weaver. I want to get my old loom working again. Do you know anyone around who might do?"

Almost without hesitation, his friend said, "No." Then after a pause, he added, "But if I hear of anyone, I'll send him to you."

Riding away from Frank's mill, Charles regretted talking of their meetings with the stewards, which had clearly alarmed Frank.

Later in the day, he met more old contacts in the cloth trade, but took care not to talk so freely again.

Towards the middle of the day, later that week, two bullock wagons loaded with wool turned into the yard beside the house. The drovers had spent the better part of three days travelling and were glad to stop. The bullocks were unhitched and allowed to graze while the drovers came into the house for a feed and a hot drink. They would not stop long, and soon set to unloading the wool, with the help of Albert and his two men.

As soon as the last load had been stacked in the dry, they brought the bullocks in and hitched them up to the wagons. Ethel took them some fresh bread and cheese to help them on their journey, and they headed off home for Dorset at a steady two miles an hour.

Albert now had to get the wool out to certain families in the village for spinning. Some of them had not had any work since the mill shut down at the time of the rebellion, so were quite pleased to see Albert.

"Perhaps now we can get back to normal again," was a comment he heard many times that afternoon.

Later that week, the blacksmith arrived and carried out a repair to the weaving loom. Though his main work was shoeing horses and bullocks, he was often called out to do emergency repairs, but on this occasion, he was not allowed to leave before the loom was tested.

Once the water level in the leet had been brought up to working level and allowed to flow over the top of the wheel, they were connected to power again. The big old loom was turned on, and the fearful racket frightened starlings and a few rats out of the building. Albert studied the clattering old loom for a few minutes till he was satisfied it was working properly. He said little but was pleased with progress and had a feeling that the mill would soon be working again.

CHAPTER EIGHT

Life at Sea.

For three weeks, Cedric worked in the broker's office in Southampton without pay, though he was housed well enough.

Late in the afternoon one day, he was strolling along the waterfront when he saw Jolecia nudging slowly alongside. Two young crewmen recognised him and shouted something unintelligible, but he waved in return; he could not conceal his delight.

Cedric returned to the office to collect his few belongings and explain that he was now returning to his ship. The crew were getting ready to load wool when he came aboard and, with luck, would get off on the next tide, so there was little time to talk. He joined in with the work, chatting with the crew when there was time to draw breath.

The skipper spoke to the mate. "We could get off on this tide, if we are quick enough.

There'll be a small bonus when it comes to payday." And that was all that was needed; the men raced to ensure that the extra payment was safe, and there was a mad rush to cast off on falling water. The skipper knew the channels out of Southampton and was observed carefully by the mate and Cedric, who watched his seamanship admiringly, storing the knowledge somewhere at the back of their brains. In deeper water, he handed over to the mate, then, turning to Cedric, he said, "You can share with the mate. There are two bunks in his cabin."

A few hours later, the skipper relieved the mate, and Cedric joined him, keen to take the tiller. After watching for a while and making a few suggestions, the skipper wandered off, though Cedric knew not where.

They chatted occasionally through the night, and Cedric learned that this cargo of wool from Southampton was bound for Calais, and they would return empty into the London Wool Wharf, hoping for another profitable load back into Southampton.

Cedric wondered if they might have an evening in the stews. He would like to know why his message had not reached his family. And though he may not have fully understood it yet, he really wanted to see Jane again.

When, after a quick turnaround in Calais they arrived in London, they discovered there was a load of wool waiting to be taken to Southampton. The skipper retained the bonus until they got to Southampton, ensuring that the crew would be ready to load wool in the morning. In the meantime, they all made their way to the stews, except for the mate, who would protect the ship.

They sat down with their first drink of the evening, a little awkwardly, as the skipper had joined them. Only when Madame had put her head around the door and beckoned him to follow her did the crew relax. Cedric was looking around intently but saw no sign of Jane; girls were going up the stairs and coming down again, and when some of them were returning a second time, he realised she was probably not working that evening.

Later, when Madame returned alone, Cedric stood up to speak to her and asked for Jane.

"Oh, I thought it was me you wanted."

He responded to her smile and replied, "Well of course I do, but I wouldn't want to offend the skipper."

She laughed. "Very sensible. Jane is not in tonight; in fact, she has not been in for a few weeks."

"Do you expect to see her again?"

"Girls are a bit of a law unto themselves. Alice, bring Cedric a drink, would you? You might like Alice; this is her first night."

When Alice returned, Cedric asked her if she would like a drink too, and they took them upstairs. Cedric spoke to her, but she seemed a bit tongue-tied, so he thought she might be a bit nervous.

"Madame told me this was your first night," he said gently.

Alice put her hand over mouth to stifle a cough and nodded her head.

"Well, let's drink to a new friendship."

"Oh, that's a nice idea, I like that."

Cedric asked if Alice knew Jane, but she replied that she knew no one here except Madame, which at least was true.

Downstairs with the crew, the evening passed in an increasingly alcoholic haze.

"Well, we got work in the morning," said someone, much later. Slowly they emptied their pots of ale and said goodnight to the girls, who invited them back when they had some more money.

After they had loaded, there were a couple of hours before the tide turned, so the crew were allowed off. The mate went ashore this time, so Cedric remained with the ship. He moved around the ship to pass the time, checking the hold was secure and that sea water would not be able to spoil the wool. He checked the lines for wear, and the main sail. The boat was rising on the tide now, and he saw he might soon have to let out the lines and move the gang plank.

The crew straggled back, followed by the skipper and the mate. There was an approving nod from the skipper, who noticed that the boat was lying easily against the quay. Within the hour they were under way, moving slowly past the Tower. Their speed increased with the falling tide as they got away from the city, heading for Gravesend and the Medway.

They headed off into the English Channel, keeping well clear of the Goodwin Sands. The skipper said he could remember when it was an island and he had seen sheep grazing there, though Cedric and the mate thought it must have been a long time ago. The skipper was adamant. "We've had some wild storms round here, in my time, which have washed a lot of it away."

After a slow journey against an unfriendly breeze, they slid between the Isle of Wight and the mainland, thankful for the half tides, which reduced the usual delays. It was too late in the day for unloading, so the crew wanted to go ashore with the promised bonus. The skipper advised them to put it away for a rainy day.

Later, after they had gone ashore, the skipper sighed, "I know that advice has already been forgotten."

The profitable three-legged journey to Calais, the London Wool Wharf and Southampton continued for many months, but when it came to an end, there was a return to the routine London to Calais trade. Sometimes Cedric hoped they might get another journey across the Mediterranean, and once spoke fondly of his first experience to the skipper, who replied, "There aren't many jobs like that one, and I'm not sure if this little boat should be out in the Atlantic at all. Now, those Portuguese boats we sometimes see in Southampton, they are the thing for big seas."

The run to Calais was short and predictable, as far as the sea can ever by predictable; unhelpful winds in the outward direction were usually favourable for the return a few hours later. Savage storms might be sat out for a couple of days in any suitable harbour, though the skipper's mood was always tense as he counted the financial loss to himself and the boat owners. If the crew could get ashore, there was the bonus of exploring the local drinking places, and they were so much bolder as a group; a few drinks and their confidence knew no limits. Idiotic behaviour might then lead to them being thrown out on to the street, but generally the setback was shared cheerfully enough. For some of the crew, this small boat was their only family; a feeling which intensified over a period of months. Cedric, who thought about his family at White Clyffe with a sense of affection but now knew he could not live in the village again, already felt quite comfortable as part of the team.

An unexpected journey up the east coast to Suffolk was an enjoyable relief from the routine trade. They made their way up the River Deben to Woodbridge to collect a load of wool to take back to the wool wharf, where a broker hoped the higher prices of London might make it worthwhile. The crew enjoyed the visit to a new port, and though they found the local ale was all right after you got used to it, they also complained that there were too many good Catholic girls in Woodbridge altogether.

Their next visit to the stews was all the more enjoyable for their period of enforced celibacy in Suffolk. Cedric, too, was becoming accustomed to the regular visits, lewd conversations, and increasingly heavy drinking. He discovered that the somewhat impersonal sexual encounters were more easily managed after three or four drinks. By then, his tongue had been loosened, and he had the confidence to try to get to know the girls better... though this was not always well received.

"How did you get started in this trade?"

"I needed the money, of course."

"But the first time you did it for money, was that difficult?"

"No, it was better than not getting paid."

After that discouraging response, Cedric avoided attempts at further intimacy and drank a little more before making his way up the stairs; perhaps a little too much, on one occasion, for he lay on the bed, watching the girl undress.

"I hope you are not expecting me to undress you as well?"

"I just like watching you."

"Well, it's double time if you go over twenty minutes."

A few minutes later, he stroked her hips lightly and said, "You don't take long to be ready."

"Well, you are my fourth one in two hours."

"Do you get any pleasure?"

"Don't be silly."

"I just want to know what it's like for you."

"Are you looking for romance? You need a girlfriend, or a wife, even."

"What do you look for in a man?"

"I prefer one who doesn't ask too many questions."

*　　　*　　　*

The weeks became months, and the months became a year, and most ports along the south coast were visited from time to time. The crew hardly changed over the next year, and team spirit was strong enough to contain occasional disagreements. The skipper, who disappeared below as much as possible, soon sensed the need for a bit of brisk discipline when this happened, and if this seemed unfair and he became the focus of resentment, it served his purpose. Though if this did not work, a bit of communal deck scrubbing for the entire crew between ports might be tried.

But even the skipper was not invincible, and his age was slowly taking a toll on his body. He often had to pause for breath when coming up the ladder from his cabin. Yet his brain was still quick enough, and his eye still spotted the chance of a bargain in foreign ports, for anything that seemed cheap against London prices. A quick calculation of the currency rates led naturally to a lengthy haggle requiring additional discount for a bulk purchase.

One day, as they were returning to London on a falling tide, the skipper was rubbing his chest while talking to the mate and Cedric.

"I think I'll just go below for a bit, boys."

"You all right, Skipper?" asked the mate.

"Oh. Just a bit of indigestion, I daresay."

The incoming tide slackened, and though a light wind gave them a little progress, they could not make it to the wool wharf. On the turn of the tide, they had no choice but to anchor up on the tidal river and prepare for a long wait, while sitting tantalisingly close. The mate suggested that Cedric let the skipper know the situation.

After several minutes, Cedric returned, looking a bit uncertain.

"I've knocked several times, but he has not answered, and the door is locked."

"Oh, well, let's let him sleep on for a bit. There is nothing we can do against the tide now, anyway. We might as well settle down ourselves for a bit. Post a lookout, Cedric, and change after two hours. There'll be boats coming out of London soon."

They settled down to eat and drink and, after half an hour in the afternoon sun, several of the crew were nodding off, as was the mate, for a short while. He awoke with a start, not knowing how long he had slept, but immediately remembered the skipper. He descended the ladder quite quickly and hammered on the door, but there was no response.

The mate came back up on deck, looking quite worried. "We'll have to force the door and make sure he is well."

Returning again to the cabin with a big hammer and some tools, the crew managed to prise the door open, after a struggle. Even the noise they had made had not disturbed the skipper, so they were beginning to fear the worst.

The mate went inside alone, soon returning to the group at the door. "He's gone, he's gone. I can't believe it. His body is cold."

The crew were shocked and saddened, but soon began to wonder how they would be paid and how long their jobs would last. And still there was nothing they could do but wait for the tide.

On arrival at the London Wool Wharf, the port authorities came on board and were shown to the skipper's cabin. Quite quickly, arrangements were made to take him ashore.

The mate and Cedric went to the broker to explain the situation and came away with instructions to continue working the short trips to Calais until someone told them to stop. The broker would contact the boat owners and the skipper's family and decide what should be done with the boat.

Returning to the wool wharf, they logged Jolecia in the order for loading and waited for instructions.

Late in the day, they were told to load early next morning, allowing the crew to spend the night ashore. They wandered aimlessly in twos and threes up Tower Hill, away from the river to Old Jewry and Aldgate — no one had the stomach for the stews — and after a couple of beers, they were back on board for an early night.

Loading wool early next morning was a relief, and the work proceeded smoothly and quietly. Before long, Madame came aboard and spoke to the mate and Cedric, her careful manner concealing her feelings, for the skipper had been a friend for many years. But she offered support to the two young men, who now had responsibility for the crew and Jolecia.

"You must come in and see me in a week or two, and we'll drink to his memory."

Jolecia continued to make her way to and from Calais for weeks, then months. The mate was promoted to the skipper, and Cedric became the mate. The broker paid the crew monthly in arrears and carried out the instructions of the boat owner.

Jolecia was offered for sale in good working order, and notices were posted at the London Wool Wharf. Within a few weeks, potential buyers came aboard to inspect her; then went away again. Interest waned, and the asking price was reduced. Some repairs were carried out, and the new skipper was instructed to bring Jolecia into London in smart and shipshape condition. After six months, the owners were advised that the boat was no longer in good order, and that they should consider a refit.

Then, on what proved to be her last journey, she was taken to a yard at Gravesend for inspection. The skipper and crew were returned to London by the boatyard men and went to see the broker.

The broker spoke to the new skipper and Cedric privately. "I am afraid that is probably her last journey. Full repair would be too expensive, so she will be taken apart and they'll use what they can to repair other boats. There's plenty of work here for you two, and I think most of the crew will find something."

The broker paid them all off and left them to their own devices. It was getting a bit late in the day, and they thought perhaps they would wait till morning to see what work might be available.

CHAPTER NINE

Family Life Again.

The poor widow is alone again, having lived with the cheese buyer while her daughters had obtained work in Bridgewater. The cheese buyer had drowned when his horses bolted over a rickety bridge across the Parrett. The wagon had been smashed to pieces, the cheese swept away in the river, and her man's body was never recovered. The horses were found patiently grazing, the shafts of the wagon still attached.

He had been a kind man, and she was angry that he was dead; he deserved a few years of contentment with her. Indeed, they both deserved it. But there it was. Life must go on, and her cows must be milked twice this day, and the next.

Emma, who must have been concerned for her mother, visited every Sunday for a few weeks and remained as late as she possibly could before the long walk back into Bridgewater.

For the rest of the winter and throughout the lovely spring days, one or other of the daughters came back to the farm each Sunday. Sometimes they arrived together, and the little cottage seemed full to bursting; laughter and talk all the more uplifting after days of silence.

Emma seemed particularly contented and appeared to be putting on a bit of weight. Her breasts were full, and her hair had an unusual gleam. After her long walk, she sat peacefully and chatted idly about this and that, and it was just a comfort to be together.

Later they went out to look at the animals in the paddock beside the cottage; her revived mother soon suggested, "Let's bring those sheep in. The lambs need their tails docked before they become dirty, and there are two boys among them that need to be cut."

It was not especially strenuous, but Emma was puffing a bit and her back was aching before the job was complete. Her mother was completely focused on the work in hand and seemed not to notice Emma's discomfort.

Two weeks later, Emma told her mother she was pregnant. The walk from Bridgewater was becoming an effort, and she must either remain in Bridgewater or give up her job and return to the little farm for a few months.

Her mother responded with the obvious question, "Who is the father?" but Emma did not know and appeared not to care.

"I only ever saw him once. But he was ever so nice."

"Well, of course you can come back here, and will have to give up your job wherever you live, I suppose. I'll enjoy the company, and you can help with the work."

Emma's mother was in an unusually good mood, for she had also met someone who was ever so nice, though she had discouraged him from calling on a Sunday. He had only called in to her farm in the first place when his horse had gone lame to ask if he could leave the gelding for a few days while he walked back to his village. She had held the horse's head while he lifted his foot. There had been a nasty cut.

"I 'spect a couple of days' rest will do it, now we've got rid of the stone. Can I leave him here?"

"Well, I could do with a strong young man for a couple of jobs. But come in and have a drink first."

Time passed quite quickly while they were talking, and it was really too late in the day to do any of the jobs she had in mind.

"Look, you've got quite a good way to walk home before dark. Why don't you come over in the morning when there's more time?" And as she spoke, she put her arm around him and gave him a friendly squeeze. Unfortunately, she pulled him so tightly towards her that her breasts were squashed quite firmly against his hard, muscular, young body. Then he smiled; a smile so warm she felt obliged to kiss him lightly on the cheek.

Over the next few weeks, Young Jack repaired the fences that had not been properly maintained since her husband had died four years before. As soon as the lameness cleared up, he rode his horse to and fro, and this gave him a longer day; though his father was soon demanding he spend a bit more time on their own farm and a bit less with the good-natured widow. Young Jack felt his father was not unreasonable, and after all, he had completed the repairs to the rickety old fencing. Furthermore, with Emma living at home, there were few opportunities to be alone together.

However, Young Jack joined in with the haymaking towards the end of June, as did a number of villagers. This was quite a regular mid-summer social event in the village, when farming families were often supported by extended family and friends.

Later in the year, Emma was able to leave the baby with her mother, then had taken work locally in the village. It was not long before Young Jack called by to see how the fencing was standing up to wear and tear. The tender widow was both pleased and amused to see him.

"I heard you were courting the neighbouring farmer's daughter."

"Oh, she's a nice young girl. I've known her for years."

"Come on, you've got your eye on that bit of land that belongs to her old father, right next your father's land, haven't you?"

"Well, it might work out one day."

"Oh, well, you better come in out of sight while I try to think of some work for you to do. If you stay out there, all the village will know your business."

Emma came home every evening after work to be with her baby and left quite early in the morning, but the desire for better paid work and more independence drew her back to Bridgewater as soon as the baby was old enough to be left with her grandmother.

Young Jack and the kindly widow enjoyed the freedom for a few months, but then she had to tell him, "Our Lizzie is now pregnant and will be staying here in a couple of months."

"Oh well, if this is going to continue, first one then the other, I am just going to have to get married; but not quite yet, Oh Lord."

Two babies in the house transformed the widow's daily routine, and she was relieved to sell one of her cows; milking only two cows each day made an immediate difference. The drudgery of cheese making each day for seven or eight months was also eased now that there was less milk. She developed an ability to watch the little ones while managing the cheese with only half of her attention. The days were long, with two little ones to care for, in addition to the demands of the animals outside.

As the weeks passed, Lizzie was soon able to help, allowing her mother to sit down for a few minutes.

They all looked forward to Emma's visits most Sundays, though she had no way of sending a message when she could not come, so the fruitless wait was a torture that had to be borne; the sturdy three-year-old was slowly coming to depend more on her ever-present grandmother. But when Emma did appear, the exhilaration was even more intense. Soon, her daughter was able to out-run her grandma and leap into Emma's arms.

Living in a house full of young children and enjoying the company of their mothers, the widow was too busy and happy to be lonely.

Young Jack had taken his bride, with the convenient parcel of land so close to his father's farm. The widow accepted the inevitability of this with good humour, though retained the fondest memories of that healthy and vigorous young man.

Other men offered to help the widow with the heavy work on her farm, but she was not stirred by any of them; her life was full. They did their work and she thanked them and wished them well... except for a new cheese buyer from another district, but he did not call often, and the house was so full, and they were never alone together, so really there was no possibility of anything developing. Yet sometimes, when lying awake in the dark, the widow's thoughts strayed, and it was surprising how often she imagined herself in the cheese buyer's arms.

Chapter Ten

Ashore in Salisbury.

Cedric found work on another boat quite quickly, but it never felt the same as his first boat; there just wasn't the sense of family. He missed the old skipper, who had become a second father. Still, he persevered for quite a few months.

When in Southampton, Cedric went to see the broker for whom he had once worked free of charge. They discussed the situation; the broker knew Cedric to be reliable and trustworthy but needed time to consider what he might offer him. "Come back in the morning and we'll talk about it some more."

Cedric settled into life ashore — indeed, was stimulated by the challenge of learning new skills and procedures — and his practical experience of shipping gave him a good start. He felt safe in Southampton, far enough from Salisbury, the scene of his arrest and interrogation.

Months passed. The days grew shorter, and it had to be admitted that they passed more slowly. Cedric went to work in the dark and left in the dark.

But as spring approached, more suppliers came into the yard with samples of woven cloth, seeking new outlets, and a better price, perhaps.

One morning, a well-spoken man appeared. Cedric had an uncanny feeling he might have seen this man before, but could not sort out his memories from the jumble of events of the last few years. They chatted pleasantly about the current market for cloth, and after a discussion with the broker in the back room, Cedric returned with a price. Three weeks later, Charles arrived with a bullock wagon loaded with cloth.

Cedric and the broker inspected the woven cloth, communicating mostly by silent nods of the head. Once they were happy with the quality, the drover was instructed to move his wagon to the warehouse, where he would be helped to unload, while Cedric and Charles completed the process in the office.

It had been a long day, with an early start, and Charles was ready for a meal. Cedric accompanied him to an alehouse, which he knew would have a stable for Charles' horse and provide an adequate meal.

As they settled down with a drink and waited for their food, the conversation turned from cloth to wool, and then to sheep. Cedric reminisced about working with his father's sheep, then his experience with a local weaver in Calne.

Charles remarked, "It's a long way from the farm to a life at sea."

Cedric agreed. "Yes, sometimes it is strange how things come about."

"Do you manage to see your family much?"

"No, I haven't for a few years. We were on the London to Calais run for much of the time, so there was no opportunity to get back to Calne."

"Well, you should find it a bit easier to get from Southampton to Calne."

Cedric nodded and concentrated on chewing quite a tough piece of beef that really needed the whole of his attention. Charles noticed that Cedric was not keen to talk about his family but thought it better not to probe.

The business arrangement worked well, and Charles returned with another load of cloth almost every month.

Over time, Cedric began to trust Charles as he got to know him better. One day, he asked, "How are things in Salisbury now?"

"What do you mean? Business is busy."

"Are the military still as active as they were when I was last there?"

Guessing that Cedric was referring to the Peasants' Revolt, Charles answered, "It's much quieter now. There was no serious rioting, and no one was killed, except by the military."

"Well, I'm glad to learn that. But I must get back to my room now. Might see you in the morning, before you go."

Later in the year, Charles asked Cedric if he was happy working in Southampton or if he would prefer to work for him in Salisbury.

"You would be closer to your family, and I like the look of you. You're a smart young feller. I could almost believe you might have served in the navy."

Cedric looked straight at him. "Yes, but is it really safe yet?"

"The military have reduced the numbers from a few years ago."

Cedric was silent.

Charles waited, then smiled.

"I expect you are more interested in the position I have. There is a lot of travelling, buying wool, putting the work out to spinners then weavers, then getting the cloth to market. I need someone young and bright. And I think you have a good background in the cloth trade."

A few weeks later, Cedric was shown to Charles' private quarters in Salisbury by someone who seemed vaguely familiar. After a few minutes, Charles came out to meet Cedric.

"You know... I remember a very small woman searching for her nephew. I hope she found him."

Cedric nodded but said nothing.

He enjoyed the greater variety of his work, and the travelling too was an attractive variation from work in the city.

Charles wanted to attend a wool sale at Marlborough and thought Cedric should come with him. "After the sale, you could ride to Calne to see your family for a few days."

"Thank you, Charles. I really must see them again."

They rode north out of Salisbury, stopping to eat after a few hours. Perhaps leaving Salisbury freed Cedric's tongue. He began to talk about his life at sea with the old skipper, and his time in France.

"How did you come to be captured by the French?"

After a pause, Cedric came to the decision to tell him the story of his arrest in Salisbury during the Peasants' Revolt, the interrogation, the brutality, and the transfer to a ship commandeered by the king for naval duties.

"So, as I suspected, the little old lady was your aunt?"

"Aunt Edith. She comes to Salisbury frequently to buy wine and quality woollens for sale in the market towns near Calne."

"You might bump into her again in Salisbury."

"Yes, I hope so, though she is quite a good age."

Charles was a bit disappointed by the small quantities of wool offered for sale at Marlborough but bought enough for a single wagon load. "It was a bit expensive I think. Just not enough to choose from, which is a pity. I wonder what Warminster would be like."

Cedric did not know, but thought Warminster was best known as a grain market.

Charles nodded. "Yes, I think it is. Still, I might go home that way. I might meet someone useful."

*   *   *

Peronell had been turning cheese for two hours and felt she must get outside and rest her aching arms; it was such a monotonous labour. When she emerged into sunlight, she found her brothers talking to a man on a fine horse; her brothers were quite excited and unusually talkative.

She moved closer, then she saw Cedric. "Oh my God, Cedric! Where did you get that beautiful mare?"

"Hello, Nell, good to see you again. I did not think it would be four years, when I left Edith's cottage, before we met again."

"Well, we haven't stopped thinking about you. So where have you been all this time?"

"Oh, I've been at sea most of the time, but have worked in Southampton and Salisbury for the last few months, and this fine mare comes with the job."

"Well, you better get down and give her a rub before she takes a chill. You've given her a hard ride."

"I was keen to see you again after all this time."

Once the horse had been seen to, they moved towards the house.

"So, how is everyone?"

"Father is fine, though Mother is quite forgetful and a bit difficult, I suppose. Mind your head as you go through the door."

It took a moment or two to adjust to the dim light, then Cedric saw his father, who demanded, "What's this I hear? Arriving on a fine horse! I thought someone was coming to collect the rent, though it is the wrong time of year."

He struggled to his feet and hugged Cedric.

"Everything going well here then, Dad?"

"Yea, we go on steady. So, you have given up on life at sea, then?"

"The old skipper died on the first boat, and it has just not been the same again. So, I came ashore and am working with someone who knows Edith."

"Oh, ah, Edith, yeah… I suppose no one has told you she's been gone these two years or more. No way could you have heard."

"I think she spent a lot of time looking for me," Cedric sighed heavily. "I wish I could thank her."

Morris cleared his throat lengthily, then rubbed his nose. "They'll be bringing the cows in for milking, directly. Go and have a look at them. I'd like to know what you think."

Cedric moved towards the door and rapped his head on the lintel.

"Oh, mind your head, Cedric."

"Maybe I will, next time."

Stepping outside into bright sunshine, he took a few moments to adjust, then saw the cows coming in, with the girls ambling behind them. He leant against the wooden rail fence as they approached, now enjoying the comfortable routine of the dairy farm. The cows were content until someone broke their routine. The calves, six months old, called from a distant field, but the cows were intent on getting rid of the weight in their udders and a feed of crushed oats, and completely ignored them.

Soon, two cows were tied to the fence and eating their oats. The youngest girl, Alice, was balancing on a one-legged stool and drawing milk into the bucket with a long steady rhythm. A shallow froth sat on the surface of the milk, and the bucket was tilted to the cow's udder between her knees.

Peronell was milking the second cow nearby, a bit nervously, for a few days earlier, she had been stepped on by an irritable cow, and her toe was still quite painful. Her placid younger sister never seemed to have problems with the cows, as if her calm nature soothed the farm animals.

Peronell was not really well-suited to farming life and was happier on her weekly visits to Calne market. Sometimes she helped her cousins at Devizes and Chippenham, especially since the death of Edith, when they were glad of another pair of hands. She had noticed a tall, slim young man at Devizes, but he was terribly shy and tongue-tied. Once she sold him a dozen eggs, but he would still not open up, even in response to her most dazzling smile.

A few weeks later, he came near her stall, and she seized the initiative. "Hello, again. Have you used up all those eggs already? What did you do with them?"

"Oh, we gave them away to a family with sickly children."

"Gave them away?"

His face flushed, and he turned away in confusion. Peronell was sorry and would have spoken more gently if she had only foreseen the effect.

She did not see him again on later visits to Devizes market and was sorry she had frightened him away. He was more attractive than the pushy young men from the castle, who seemed to expect everyone to respond gratefully. Peronell knew she was attractive and had developed quite a skill for cheeky put-downs; the smart young men just lapped it up. But they were all talk, and did not buy, much to her cousin's deep disappointment.

"Better not to attract that sort, Nell. They keep the real customers away while they hang around here."

Returning to Calne at the end of the day, her cousin said he might have to miss Devizes next week as he would be going to Salisbury to buy stock.

"Oh, can I come with you? I'd like to see Cedric again."

"Well, I suppose so. Will your father mind?"

Almost a week later, they set off from Calne before daybreak for the long journey to Salisbury. The little town was still, and no one stirred as they made their way eastwards towards Blackland Hollow; a formidable climb to the Marlborough Downs. Good time was made across the top, and they came down into Bishop's Cannings just as the sun emerged into a pale sky. From here, it was an easy run for the horses across the Pewsey Vale, and they reached the valley of the Avon well before mid-day. In another hour, they found the outskirts of Salisbury.

"Do you know where Cedric lives?"

"No, but I know the mill where he works when he is not travelling."

They pulled into the yard at the mill. Peronell's cousin called out, "We are looking for Cedric!" and paused while a blank-faced young man struggled to frame a reply.

"I want Cedric Johnson, is he here?"

"Oh, I dunno. Thee better look inside. Pr'aps 'e be."

Cedric could not be found inside the mill, or out.

After a persistent search, someone went to Mister Charles, who came down to see who was making such a fuss about Cedric. He walked slowly towards the small group, looking none too pleased to be disturbed. Before he could speak, Peronell stepped forward with a glorious smile.

"Oh, I am so sorry to be a nuisance, but I am looking for my brother, Cedric. Does he still work here?"

"I'm pleased to say he does, though he will not return for two days at least."

Peronell was downcast at once, her face a scene of desolation.

"Oh, what can we do? I so want to see him again." Her voice faltered and her eyes might have overflowed with tears at any moment.

Her cousin sought to calm her. "Look, you can return to Calne with me and come back to Salisbury again, the next time we need to buy more supplies."

"Oh, but it will be weeks and weeks before you return, and even then, Cedric might not be here."

Poor Charles, essentially a kind-hearted man, could not allow this sad, beautiful girl to suffer so. "We've plenty of room here. You can stay for a couple of nights till Cedric returns."

Later that night, they ate in the city. Peronell positively glowed in the company of the smart, older man. He asked after her father and the family, which set her at ease from the start. Peronell spoke of her admiration of Cedric when he had arrived at the farm on his fine white horse, and how they had laughed when her father had pretended to think he had come to collect the rent.

"Does he travel much in his work?"

"Yes, we both do. Though there is less pressure on me now that I can share the work with Cedric. But we need to find our suitable supplies of wool, then send it out to the spinners and weavers. Then we often go down to Southampton to the broker with the finished cloth."

It was a warm evening, and they strolled through the city.

"Perhaps you will have time to do more of this, now that Cedric is helping you."

"Yes, but it is far more enjoyable with a companion."

Peronell remained silent but slipped her arm through his.

*   *   *

Late on the third day, a tired horseman returned. Cedric led the mare into the stable and removed the harness, then secured her with a light halter. The groom had still not appeared, so he began to rub down the steaming horse before she might take a chill. A close bond was forming between them, and she nuzzled him softly. Cedric lowered his head to breathe into her nostrils. Not till he was satisfied she had cooled down did Cedric make his way into the mill.

Charles met him on the upper floor. "We have a visitor for you, Cedric."

He stepped aside and revealed Peronell, who rushed forward to hug Cedric. "I am so pleased to see you after all these weeks. And it is so quiet on the farm, so here I am!"

If she expected a warm response, she must have been disappointed. Cedric seemed stunned, and could not find words, or sort out the jangle of questions racing through his brain.

Charles read the scene swiftly and asked how the wool sale had gone. "Oh, yea, yea, prices were reasonable. There'll be three wagon loads coming here next week."

"Ah, you'll want to get that booked in. Why don't we eat together tonight? If you come back when you've freshened up, then we'll see what we can find."

Later, when Cedric had recovered from the shock, he was more talkative.

"I guess you came down on the wagon, Nell?"

"Yes, I have been helping out at Devizes and other markets, and I dearly wanted to see what Salisbury was like. Do you remember how Grandad used to tell us about the amazing spire? It fair took my breath away when I actually saw it. I don't know how they managed to build anything so tall and slender, and why it has not fallen over."

"Well, yes, it is striking, especially when it gleams in the sun."

"Have you been inside it yet?"

"No, Charles keeps me so busy."

"Then how about this Sunday?"

"Um, I'm off to another wool sale tomorrow. With luck I may be back for Sunday."

After two pints of ale and a good meal, Cedric was struggling to keep his eyes open and contributed little more to the conversation, but Charles was quite happy to talk to Peronell.

The next morning, when Peronell rose, Cedric could not be found, and the horse had gone from the stable. She returned upstairs slightly downcast but brightened on seeing Charles.

"Have you eaten, Charles?"

"Not yet, let's eat together."

Peronell helped Charles to his breakfast and later cleared everything away. Charles was enjoying this unfamiliar luxury. Peronell chose the moment to thank him for his kindness and hospitality.

"Is there anything useful I can do for you, in return? I really would like to help."

"I am going to see some of the weavers this morning; you could take notes for me. I've noticed you can write as well as Cedric, so I'm sure you'll cope."

"Father taught us all to write, and he said his father taught him."

An hour later, Charles led Peronell down to the yard, where a pony and trap had been made ready for them. They sat together with a sheepskin rug across their knees and rattled out of the gate over cobblestones into the traffic. Charles handed the reins to Peronell. "Let's see how you get on, Nell."

She turned towards him and smiled. It was the first time he had called her Nell.

The traffic was no more difficult than Calne or Devizes, only there was more of it, and the drivers were less courteous.

"Pull in here, Nell, where you can." He had raised his voice to be heard above the awful racket from the weaving shop.

"Hold the mare here, if you can. I'll bring the weaver outside, where we can talk."

"Peronell this is John Skinner." They nodded to each other. "John has two cloths ready and may have another in a few days. If you could write that down and add the street name, so that the carrier will be able to find them?"

One weaving shop followed another throughout the day till Charles was satisfied. "Let's go home, Nell. I think we will have a full wagon load for Southampton. But we need to know which cloth came from which weaver."

The next morning, after an hour at the mill with the men, Charles returned upstairs for breakfast. After a leisurely meal, Peronell asked, "So what can I do for you today, Charles?"

"You are doing it already, Nell. I have not had this much care and comfort for a long time."

Nell remained silent, thinking he might explain his missing wife.

After a pause, he said, "Why don't we go downtown and see about some clothes?"

"I'd love that, Charles. I do feel a bit 'home-made' in my country clothes."

"I don't think you need have any doubts about your appearance. As far as I can see, all the men are envying me when I am in your company."

Several happy hours later, after looking and feeling, trying and choosing, being measured and pampered, Peronell turned to Charles and leaned into his broad chest, the whole length of her body quite relaxed. She turned her face upwards and kissed him tenderly.

Too happy to speak, they strolled back to the mill, where Nell tactfully walked behind Charles until he had closed the door of his private quarters.

"After all that, I think we both need a rest."

Charles took Nell's hand and sat her down on his bed. He knelt and removed her shoes, quite slowly, his fingertips brushing the soles of her feet. She lifted her feet, lay her head on the bed, and looked up at Charles, still standing indecisively. She reached up to touch his lips with her fingertips, and this seemed to galvanise his response. Charles' tongue seemed to surround and attempt to devour each finger, one by one.

Peronell drew him down to her level, removing his heavy outdoor coat. He responded by helping her out of her clothes, till she lay with her hands covering part of her breasts.

Charles tore off the remainder of Peronell's clothes and lay beside her in a moment. Nell slipped beneath the bed covers and Charles lay beside her. He stroked her hair and told her how beautiful she was and talked and talked, till Nell wondered who had to make the first move. Somewhat stealthily, she traced the hairs on his chest with a long finger, down over his hard muscular belly, and still he talked. Not till she took hold of his penis was he interrupted.

"Jesus Christ."

"Oh, please dear lord, be gentle."

Unknown hours later, Charles stirred briefly. It was already dark. He listened to Peronell's soft breathing and was gone again.

As the room lightened, yet later, he woke again, moving slowly and carefully, hoping not to disturb Peronell, and left the room.

She woke as he returned. "I've been dreaming about you."

"A happy dream, I hope."

Charles slipped back into bed, lightly brushing Peronell's hair back from her face. He kissed her as her soft, limp arm lay on his shoulders.

For an hour they were joined together, till his conscience got the better of him.

"I wonder if anyone is working in the mill."

"They might be doing what we are doing."

"They'd better not be. Not on my time."

Peronell giggled happily.

CHAPTER ELEVEN

The Past Returns.

In a quiet, anonymous street, a man alone in his house stares morosely at a blank wall. His masters demand more and pay him less; now they expect him to find out who travels regularly from Salisbury to the port at Southampton. And they demand to know the purpose of these journeys. It was so much simpler during the rebellion, when the agitators were easily seen, as if they had no fear; some even posted notices in broad daylight. And the military, in their panic, paid well for any scrap of knowledge.

Now, after sifting through acres of useless city gossip, they are more discerning, their targets more precise. They had found no one who had led or co-ordinated the revolt in Salisbury. It appeared to have been a completely spontaneous movement, which the military could not believe, for the peasants had always been resentful, to no effect. So why had there been an explosion, on this occasion, and why, on this single occasion, had it spread like fire on a blistering wind from east to west? There must have been an established organisation in place, perhaps, even now, lying in wait to unleash another revolt. Who were these people, who could move from place to place in the normal course of their daily work?

He rose stiffly, dressed for rain, and left the house. In less than an hour he had reached the outskirts of Salisbury and was on the road for Southampton. There was no traffic — he was too early — but relentlessly he continued till first light.

Beside the road, in the yard of an alehouse, drovers were watering their oxen before hitching them to wagons or carts. Of course, this was the place to collect the information. Who did he have who worked in an alehouse, or who could be placed in one of the alehouses along this road? And which would be the best and busiest?

He walked till mid-day, then, exhausted, he stopped, in genuine need of refreshment.

There were few people in the bar, eating or drinking, and he could not get into a conversation; perhaps it was his precise questioning style. He was, after all, more accustomed to interrogation and bullying. But he knew this; he knew he must use other people to obtain the insignificant details that, collectively, might build a picture.

He heaved himself reluctantly from the wooden bench, took himself outside, and turned for Salisbury.

*　　　*　　　*

Charles, from time to time, returned to Bridgewater to oversee his original business to support his wife, Ethel, and to assist Albert, who had the burden of keeping it all going. He had to admit to himself that the intervals between visits to Somerset were growing longer, and now that he had met Peronnell, he really did not want to go at all. But he must; he simply must keep up appearances, to encourage Albert, at the very least. Soon he might be able to send Cedric in his place, who had already ridden to Bridgewater with messages, and when better known to Albert and Ethel, might be accepted as a substitute.

Charles arrived at the mill ringing wet, muddy, and exhausted. He dismounted in the yard and led his horse into the stable, where a young mill worker helped him remove the saddle and bridle. With a light halter, he walked her around the yard a few times, then allowed her to drink. Charles gave her a bit more quiet exercise, then brought her back into the stable for a feed. Only then could he think about getting changed out of his travelling clothes and kicking off his boots before the fire.

He had arrived late in the day, and Ethel, Albert, and Albert's niece were already enjoying their evening meal; indeed, Albert was almost asleep. No one had noticed his arrival in the yard, which was quite unexpected.

Albert was the first to speak, as ever; pleased to see Charles again. Ethel slowly moved to see what she might be able to give Charles to eat, but he sought to stop her. "No, stay where you are and put your feet up. I can grab something when I've got cleaned up." He was mildly surprised to see her settle again next to Albert, relaxed and comfortable beside each other.

The next morning, the day was fine, and all were in the yard quite early. Albert had everyone at work and looking busy before Charles emerged. Albert then led him around the mill to admire the quality of the latest weaving, before drawing his attention to some repairs that he thought needed urgent attention. As they emerged from the building, Ethel came from the house with two heavy buckets full of wastewater.

"Yer, let I 'ave they, missus," said Albert, and she put them down gratefully, with a little smile.

Later in the day, Charles and Edith had a few moments alone together. Charles thought Albert was managing so well and dealing with everything that came along each day that he should be paid better. Ethel was cautious. "We are just getting back on our feet now. Let's have a full year of profit before we start giving it away. And there might be a downturn at any stage."

Charles was inclined to agree that trade could turn down without warning. "Perhaps if we give him a slice from each sale, then when the price falls, or we don't find a sale for a few months, we'll be protected?"

Most days, Charles rode out to Bridgewater, or to see old clothier friends in nearby villages. They would chat about current problems; usually the shortage of skilled workers, or the difficulty of finding good quality wool. Generally, those producing un-dyed wool for the export trade were quietly confident. However, this trade demanded the finest wool, leaving quite a lot of poorer quality wool which must be used to supply the local market. Ironically, the finest wool came from the thinnest pastures on the Mendips, the Marlborough Downs or the

Cotswold Hills, all involving long slow journeys by bullock cart.

Charles was growing older and was happy to encourage the younger clothiers to lead the way to progress. Just occasionally he might remind them of their unfulfilled ambitions to persuade the landowners and their stewards of the pressing need to make better use of the abandoned arable in the ancient cropping lands of most villages.

As the days passed, Charles' desire to return grew stronger, till he could wait no longer. He set out soon after daybreak, reaching Salisbury early on the second afternoon. On his return, he noticed one of his men in a side street beside the mill, apparently in conversation with a short, muscular man who had turned away abruptly at the sound of horse's hooves.

Something alarmed Charles. The hair on the back of his neck bristled instinctively. He rode into the yard, dismounted, and handed his horse over to a groom. His man had not yet returned from the side street, so he went out to have a look, but as he emerged from the yard, the man came towards him, doffed his hat, and passed without speaking.

After a discreet pause, Charles turned and walked back inside the mill, watching his leisurely progress across the mill. Charles did not recognise him and asked the foreman how long he had worked here.

"This is his second week. He is still settling in but seems quite useful."

"Keep an eye on him, 'specially if he goes out of the mill. I don't like that."

Then Peronell appeared and Charles' face brightened immediately. They walked to the upper floor and, when out of sight, he stroked her fingers.

"Oh, Charles, how are you? You must be tired after that long journey. Would you like a hot drink?"

She helped him out of his boots and took his riding coat.

"You found some mud to ride through. Just look at this coat!"

Charles sat down in front of the fire while Peronnell put another log on and gave it a good poke. By the time the water had boiled, he was sound asleep.

Peronell hovered, unwilling to make Charles' drink till he woke. Almost without thinking, she ran her fingers through his thinning hair. His eyelids flickered but he did not wake.

While carrying his coat and boots to dry, she made a bit more noise than intended. On her return, he was stirring. Peronell made the drink and sat on the floor beside Charles, her long, black hair just reaching his thighs.

"In all my travels, Nell, I have seen nothing as beautiful as your hair."

Nell smiled. "I have been waiting for you, hoping to see you every day, not knowing if you were even safe or well."

Charles lifted her hair and let it cascade through his fingers.

"You could be an angel."

"But I am no longer innocent enough, since meeting you."

They laughed together, and her mischievous, dancing eyes bewitched him again.

Later in the day, Cedric returned, and Charles went out to speak to him. Peronell dressed and tidied her appearance, emerging with a lovely smile.

"Hello, dear brother. Have you had a hard day's ride, too? I expect you'd both like a hot drink?"

Easily persuaded, they followed her to the inner room, where the remains of the fire needed a bit more attention.

Cedric turned to Charles. "How are things at Bridgewater?"

"Oh, Albert has things running quite smoothly. Finding a weaver was the most difficult thing, and we never found out what happened to the other one."

"Funny he never came back when things got quieter. Don't suppose he will now. How is their cloth selling?"

"There's a good demand for the un-dyed broadcloth — stronger than Salisbury Ray, I'd say. The dyers on the continent can't get enough of it."

After a short silence, Charles continued, "How did you get on in the Cotswolds a few weeks ago?"

Cedric hesitated. "The Bristol merchants have that pretty much sown up. The only wool I found in local markets wasn't good enough for them, or for us. So, I rode down to Bristol to see their wool market, which had some better wool, though I think they keep the best for their own weavers."

"Yes, that sounds about right. I expect we'll carry on buying the best of the country wool near to our mills. But it will do no harm to get to know people in Bristol. You never know when you might need some help."

"Is there enough good quality wool in Somerset for the broadcloth weavers?"

"I think so, for the time being, but it would be a good idea for you to spend a bit of time trying the markets around there next time you're down that way, Cedric."

*   *   *

Charles and Peronnell were so happy together, living only in the present, without a care for the future, and their days passed swiftly. The suspicious man left his job after a few weeks, adding to the sense of wellbeing. Cedric, after a few weeks of working locally, went looking for wool further afield, following the suggestion that he should learn a bit more about the Bristol trade.

In earlier days, Cedric had enjoyed his frequent visits to the London wool wharf in the proximity of the great wool merchants, on whom the young king depended for financial support. It excited him to be working in a large city again. A wide range of goods arrived in Bristol from northern and western Europe on large boats, using the highest tides in England.

Cedric walked along the tidal river, sometimes at low tide, when the boats sat on the mud, far below the paved road of the wharf. The first quiver of life as the incoming tide lifted the boat even an inch from the mud excited him; he would pause as she trembled from stem to stern. The strength of the incoming tide astonished him as it rushed in for several miles from the Severn through the Avon Gorge, pouring into the main wharfs of St. Augustine's Reach and the lower reaches of the diverted River Frome. Bristol Bridge across the main Avon River was a good vantage point, as the rising tide filled both the Frome and the Avon, almost surrounding the ancient city inside the walls. Cedric would return to the markets in the city invigorated and happier than he had been since his days on Jolecia with the good old skipper. Though he came to the conclusion that any Cotswold wool purchased in Bristol would require a long, slow journey by bullock cart to Salisbury and would not be worth the trouble, he could also see that there was money to be made here in the largest city after London.

For Charles and Peronell, in Salisbury, the happy months passed all too quickly, and Charles had to make another visit to the mill near Bridgewater. Peronnell hated saying goodbye to anyone, and the last days were agony. She stood forlornly, looking at his back, hoping he might turn and wave to her before he disappeared from sight.

Charles soon left Salisbury behind him and followed the valley of the River Wylye to Warminster, the route quite familiar to him now as he clattered through the streets of the old market town. Out in the countryside beyond, the bright sunshine of early morning had disappeared, concealed by an odd haze. The air was still, yet heavy and humid. The road took him through a mile of woodland, which seemed unfamiliar in dim light. So strange was it, Charles wondered if he had taken a wrong turn. When he emerged, dark clouds were bubbling and seething high in the sky before him, till he felt he was looking at an unstable mountain hanging over his head. He was apprehensive and might have taken shelter, if any could be seen.

The road descended into a valley. Charles caught a glimpse of a river through trees below him, flowing fast, brown and angry.

Huge, cold raindrops struck him with unexpected force; he slowed the horse to a walk, for he could hardly see a few feet beyond her head. The rain stopped abruptly, to be replaced with a violent wind that threatened to rip him from the saddle. Now he had to stop completely.

When the wind had weakened to the force of a severe gale, Charles edged tentatively forward, heavy rain now lashing him from behind. Though it was still early afternoon, he thought, he could not see ten yards ahead; only the lightning showed him the way.

The storm had come down to ground level and filled the valley through which Charles had to pass. Thunder crashed almost simultaneously with the lightning. The noise was deafening, though strangely the wonderful old mare was resolute, carrying them both along a rough track that had already become a second river. He did not know how long this terrifying storm would last, nor how far they had travelled. Then, Charles was confronted by a huge oak tree torn from top to bottom by a lightning strike and completely blocking the road.

He stopped; or rather the fallen tree compelled the horse to stop. They waited, the mare taking a few mouthfuls of oak leaves, without much enthusiasm. The wind dropped to a low howl among the trees, but the rain continued relentlessly, washing mud, stones, and small branches down the slope till obstructed by the fallen tree. A small dam formed against the tree, and as the water backed up the slope, Charles was forced to turn around.

He took the horse up the valley till he found an opening large enough for them both to pass. They came out into farmland, where there was just enough light to avoid the larger obstacles.

Slowly Charles' eyes adjusted, and he identified a large, black shape. As he came nearer, he sensed rather than saw that it was a farm building.

A low building with an open front at least gave cover from the terrible rain. Both man and horse, exhausted by hours of high wind, were relieved to find shelter.

Charles dismounted and removed the saddle and bridle. The mare, Bonney, sank to her knees with a grunt, falling backwards as her stiff hind legs gave way beneath her. As Charles stroked her long head and spoke to her softly, she laid her head to rest on the ground. Both, utterly spent, were either asleep or unconscious within minutes.

Bright sunlight brought both to their senses, and Bonney needed a feed before another long day. Charles led her out to graze and drink. Not far away was a small cottage, all windows tightly shuttered against the worst weather. There was no obvious sign of human life, yet Charles felt someone was watching him. He allowed Bonney to graze for a while, then took her back to the low building, where the saddle and bridle had been drying out overnight. He led Bonney by hand for the first mile so that she warmed up gradually, reducing the risk of a torn muscle.

They were moving towards Bath when they saw the first sign of flooding. Turning away to higher ground, Charles followed a muddy track to a small village where cattle had reduced the road to a quagmire. The road climbed out of the village, soon crossing a small stream. This was another opportunity to let Bonney drink while he cleaned the worst of the mud from her lower limbs.

They continued west, and around the middle of the day, rejoined the road for Bridgewater, finding an inn with stabling within a mile. Charles had not eaten for twenty-four hours, and the horse would also enjoy a bellyful of hay, so he decided to stay overnight. The fact that he was a day and a half later than his intended arrival meant nothing, since Edith and Albert had no expectation that he was on his way to visit them.

Albert was always pleased to see Charles and proud to show him how well they were doing. The two men would talk at great length about the quality of the finished cloth and the demands of the buyers of the un-dyed broadcloth. Charles was coming to the view that supplying the export trade from Bristol, which was now receiving larger boats from the continent, might be better than carting heavy loads across the country to the south coast ports. The hours passed before they knew it, and they both crept into the house to see Ethel together.

"So, you have turned up at last. I saw you come into the yard a few hours ago. I don't know what was most important to you, I am sure."

"The time just ran away from us, and we had a lot to deal with."

Ethel was not easily placated, and Charles left them together while he stripped off his riding clothes and put his bag of cash away safely. When he returned, cleaner and fresher, Ethel's mood had softened, at least towards Albert. They were talking quietly together by the fire.

Charles went across to the stable to check his horse. She, at least, was affable, and pleased to receive an armful of hay. Charles rubbed her down for a few minutes before returning to the house.

"Are you planning to eat here tonight?"

Charles nodded in response to a needless question.

"Well, you might let me know, or I might not have enough for us all."

Charles thought it wiser not to respond.

Both slept well and woke refreshed, though conversation was awkward.

Charles went out into the yard as soon as decently possible, and later in the morning, rode out of the yard without saying where he was going. Riding round the villages, the reduced areas of arable, surrounded by abandoned cropping land now infested with weeds and brambles, were an affront. Charles felt, as he had for some years, that this wasteland should be enclosed for sheep farming to produce more wool for the fast-growing cloth trade.

Over the next few days, Charles caught up with old clothier friends, their discussion turning again to the lack of progress since their aborted plans in 1381. Some of the younger ones were keen to reactivate the attempt, but not his old friend Frank, who was deeply anxious. They had a meeting, and one of the younger clothiers spoke to a steward in an alehouse who was in the area making one of his routine visits. Perhaps their conversation was overheard, but for whatever reason, two days later, Charles was picked up by the military and taken in for questioning. Though released after three days without sleep, the aggressive questioning and some decidedly rough treatment had left him badly shaken.

Charles only stayed for one night at the cloth mill and left on his horse before daybreak. He decided not to ride through Bridgewater but headed south into Dorset, returning to Salisbury from the south-west.

For three days he rode, aimlessly at times, turning over his options. He recognised that he might well be arrested again, and if he should be linked to both Bridgewater and Salisbury, his chances would be extremely poor. If further interrogation revealed his clothier colleagues in Somerset, the military might well think they had found the organisers of the Bridgewater riots.

*   *   *

Peronell saw immediately that Charles was in a poor state on his return. She looked after him tenderly and was only concerned for his comfort and wellbeing; she asked no questions, prepared to wait till he was ready to talk.

After a restful night, Charles told Nell about the terrifying and exhausting storm, and this seemed to be an adequate explanation for his weakness and exhaustion. Yet there was no recovery, and he seemed not to regain his normal humour. Charles was busy in the mill and sharp with all his dealings; he simply was not the man they had known before.

But Charles now knew what he must do, with certainty, and he would handle the consequences, however painful. He immediately set to work to close down his Salisbury business. Raw wool in store was sold for cash, spun wool was sent to the weavers, but no more raw wool went out to the spinners. Within weeks, the weavers were not used again and were paid off.

Cedric could see the signs of decline on his regular visits, and this prompted him to discuss his hopes of returning to sea, perhaps from Bristol. Charles accepted this easily, though neither discussed the run-down of the business. Cedric simply accepted that Charles would not be buying any more wool for this business. Charles said he would like to keep Cedric's horse and suggested he take another for his last journey to Bristol, which he could either sell or keep for himself. Cedric was quite pleased with this arrangement and rode out of the yard with a comforting bag full of cash. Typically, he did not say goodbye to Nell.

Charles had been silent, often anxious, since his return from Bridgewater. One evening, as they lay together, he told Peronell the business would be closed down. She should take Cedric's horse as a gift for all she had given him, and ride to her father's farm at White Clyffe. Her cousins were in town, so this was a good opportunity for her to travel safely in their company.

In the morning, he gave her a secure bag of coin as another gift. Their last night of loving had been the saddest Peronell had ever known.

"You must say nothing to anyone about my plans, but with any luck, we'll meet again, and I hope you will still be able to love me. Now I'll go down and get the horse ready for you. Just walk normally across the yard to the stable and then you will be gone before anyone knows."

Over the next week, the woven cloth was collected from the independent weavers and loaded onto the carrier's wagon. The few remaining workers in the yard were paid off. Charles walked around the building almost in a state of shock; the possibility of never seeing Nell again was the heaviest burden of all. He checked the building, secured the doors and windows, and walked to the stable, to his last faithful companion. He swung into the saddle and rode out of the yard, following the carrier's wagon to Southampton, and did not return.

CHAPTER TWELVE

Afloat Again.

Cedric and the owner of the boat take Fandangle down the Avon and out into the Severn on a falling tide. In a light westerly, they are quite unable to make any headway against the fast-flowing river, so drop anchor in flatter water, away from the main current to wait for slack water. Fandangle is a single-masted cog with a flat bottom, able to sit comfortably on the mud. Only 50ft in length, she can carry up to sixty tons, barely half the capacity of Jolecia. And Cedric has a good opportunity to study her while they sit for two hours, waiting till the main rush of water is spent. The Severn is still flowing, but much more slowly, so he has still to avoid the main current.

Later, as the rising tide comes in behind them, they make better speed. The owner points out the shallows, an area of rocks hidden by a high tide. "Plenty of boats have come to grief here, mind."

The upper river below Gloucester was narrow and twisty, and a bit tricky in a light wind, but both knew they would not come to harm on the rising tide. "Be different coming down, mind. I like to get out on the river before high tide, if I can."

In Gloucester Docks, the skipper introduced Cedric to the people he would have to deal with. "This is my new skipper; he'll be handling my business now. Same terms as ever — cash on the nail, of course, Bristol fashion." They were bringing Irish fish that had been unloaded at Bristol only a few hours earlier.

There was frequent movement between Bristol and the smaller ports of South Wales and the north coast of Somerset and Devon. Often back loads into Bristol added a double profit for the skipper, but there was nothing for them on this occasion.

On the way back to Bristol, they nudged into the approach to Lydney harbour, over on the west bank.

"You want to come in here before high tide, if you can, unload fast and get out again while there is still plenty of water. We are too late today, but it's worth a look, so you know what you have to deal with."

Cedric soon took another load to Gloucester; on this occasion, fine wines from Gascony and a return load of grain previously brought downriver from many miles upcountry.

Within a few months, he had got to know most of the ports of the Channel but had avoided the tricky approach into Bridgewater till he had become accustomed to the roaring tides.

*   *   *

Cedric had found the possessive attention and demands of both Charles and Peronell extremely wearing, and longed for the solitary life at sea, though happy with his freedom while away from the mill. He had often wandered along St Augustine's Reach when in Bristol; the smell and surge of the incoming tide cleared his irritation quite quickly, and he loved to talk to the crews as they came ashore.

Cedric gradually developed an understanding of the Bristol trade. In recent years, substantial quantities of wine and fish had come in from the Atlantic ports of France and the Bay of Biscay; increasingly more exotic goods, such as spices, arrived from the Mediterranean. These large boats came into Bristol on the highest tides in England but had to time their arrival and departure exactly.

Bristol merchants sold the greater part in the city and surrounding towns, though a significant amount was transferred quickly to smaller craft delivering to minor ports above and below the city.

One day, with time to kill, Cedric had found himself chatting to the owner of a small boat, who had returned from a short trip to Swansea. He was weary and clambered off the boat with some difficulty.

"I'm getting too old for this game. I'm going to have to sit down over there," he said, nodding to an alehouse across the road. Well, one drink led to another, and gradually each learned the life story of the other. Within a few weeks, Cedric found himself taking the trial run with his first load of Irish fish for Gloucester.

Cedric needed to keep busy and would like to be working six days a week. He was becoming known on the docks. The boat owner had worked on the river all his life, yet despite his valuable contacts, there were often gaps, when Cedric had no work. However, he had recently contacted a Somerset weaver who was selling his production to a Bristol merchant. There promised to be one or two loads per month, which should become a nice, steady job that would help to keep him busy.

It was not easy to find the entry into the Parrett between the hidden mud banks of

Bridgewater Bay, and Cedric was glad the boat was empty. He came in on a rising tide but was an hour late. With an unhelpful wind, he drifted in very slowly, as the flow of water diminished. Cedric and his crew of one managed to get the boat tied up, then he hurried to find the weaver and prepare a plan for loading. He returned after an hour to find his crewman talking to a pleasant girl.

She turned to Cedric. "Oh, hello. I'm Emma. I like to come down here to see who has arrived. I work on the other side of town, so it's nice to meet people here."

"Well, you might be able to help me. We'll need to find somewhere to eat; it's been a long day. Where do you think we should go?"

"I need to get back in time to start work, so if you walk with me, I could show you." She chattered all the way to the first alehouse. "How long will you be here for?"

"Oh, we'll be away tomorrow on the tide, after we are loaded."

Three weeks later, Cedric returned to Bridgewater to collect another load of cloth, but did not see Emma till much later, when he had completed loading and was waiting for the tide to turn. Emma then came on board, but it was chilly on deck, and they went down to the cabin to escape the wind. Emma talked away, lightly and carelessly, till it was time for her to go back to work.

The next time he arrived in port, the timing was different. He did not see Emma until he was busy loading cloth with his boy and the men who had brought the finished cloth from the mill beyond the town. It was a filthy wet day, and Cedric was worried that the tide was not far from the turn.

Emma had a sweet, gentle nature and offered to make a hot drink for them all. Cedric did not take the offer very gracefully; in fact, he was quite grudging.

Within the hour, the boat was loaded, the tide had turned, and water was distinctly flowing out of the harbour.

Cedric shouted, "Come on, come on, let's get her tied down and out of here!"

Emma wanted to stay a bit longer with him, but he was impatient. "No, you must get off now. We are leaving at once."

Emma was deeply hurt. Cedric did not even look at her, let alone wave goodbye as the boat moved away.

They did not meet the next time he came into Bridgewater, but on a later visit he saw her talking with the sailors on another boat. He controlled his feelings, walked past the boat, and headed for one of the more sociable alehouses.

The hour was late, and Cedric sat quietly drinking, alone, feeling low.

Around two o'clock in the morning, the owner of the business came to sit next to him. "We are quiet tonight. I am going to let the girls go home, unless you want anything."

There was little response, so the owner started cashing up, and the girls left the house, tightly clutching their purses. She turned to Cedric. "Well, I am going to bed. Where are you going to sleep?"

"I'm not going back to the boat tonight."

"Well, come on, then." She turned away, and he followed.

As the sun rose, a few hours later, one disturbed the other, and they lay quietly together.

"You ready to go back to the boat now?"

"'Spose I'll have to."

"Well, you don't have to go just yet."

"Oh, all right then."

Not much later, he walked back to the boat, his manly ego restored. As he reached the quay, the widow's daughter, Emma, came ashore, stumbling at precisely the right moment that he had to step forward to save her from falling. She thanked him. He continued to hold her arm.

Emma asked Cedric when he would be sailing.

"Probably won't catch tonight's tide, I don't think."

"Oh, well, might see you again, then."

There was no way of knowing when Fandangle might be in the harbour, nor how long she might stay, and though Emma might visit the harbour two or three times a week, she often missed his visits completely.

A month went by, and Emma wondered when, if ever, she might see Cedric again. She had a few hours off work and would just wander into town to see who she might bump into. Waiting to cross the busy road for a bullock wagon, she thought it was the same driver she had seen before. She followed the wagon to the harbour, and there was a boat waiting to be loaded, but it was not Fandangle.

She asked the drover if he was the same one she had seen before and he said, "I remember you made us a hot drink. 'Twas a terrible wet day. Skipper was in a bad mood though, and that didn't help."

Emma tried to suppress the awful memory, but her face conveyed the message.

"I 'spose Fandangle must be due again soon."

"Oh, you just missed her. She was in last week. Be another two weeks, I expect, before they comes again."

Downcast for a moment, Emma rallied, "How often do you bring cloth here?"

"Well, every week, I daresay; sometimes twice."

"Is that all from the same mill?"

"No, I cart for anyone who pays me."

"So, you know a few days ahead who will be coming in?"

"Well, I know I've only got one job next week, and it's not Fandangle."

"Oh, well, I might go back to see Mother this Sunday, then."

*   *   *

For many months, Cedric and Emma met occasionally, but more often they missed each other. Neither knew what to expect.

One Saturday, Cedric came in, expecting a load of wool for Bristol, but to his annoyance it was not ready and could not be expected before Monday.

He knew where Emma worked and thought she might ease his resentment. Emma was elated to see him but could not leave work for a few hours. Cedric sat quietly, eating and drinking, watching Emma manage the company with some skill, swaying easily away from would-be affectionate arms.

The next morning, they walked out to the poor widow's cottage, where Emma's daughter had grown up with her grandmother.

"She is changing so quickly now and learns new tricks so fast."

Cedric had no recent experience of family life and was unsure how to deal with such a small human being. Still, he supposed she would remain with her grandmother, as before. The cottage was quite crowded, with Emma's sister, Lizzie, and her own two-year-old daughter, Ivy, but most of the day was spent out of doors, exploring the village and surrounding farms.

Since no one had expected Emma to bring Cedric with her, the family had no time to make any special preparation, such as cleaning the cottage. However, Cedric noticed that the fencing was in good order, and said so. Emma's mother accepted this comfortably, though a wistful look passed fleetingly across her face.

Cedric was quite at home with the cows and sheep, having grown up on a dairy farm at White Clyffe, and chatted easily to Emma's mother.

Late on Sunday, Cedric and Emma walked back to Bridgewater, both needing to start work early next morning. Little Hazel walked with them as far as she could, then said goodbye without tears, for this had been her regular routine for all the time she could remember. And she loved her grandma.

Cedric and Emma turned and walked away, hand in hand. They waved goodbye and were gone.

Fandangle was lying easily against the wharf, on slack lines. There was something gently soothing about a night in a cabin afloat, at least till the tide went out and the boat was on the mud at an uncomfortable slope.

Chapter Thirteen

Survivors.

Cedric had been busy for a year, building his business out of Bristol, but occasionally his thoughts turned to Charles. He had never understood why Charles had shut his Salisbury business down in such a hurry. Perhaps the next time he was in Bridgewater, he would go out to the old mill and might meet him there. Though, on second thoughts, there was every possibility that Charles and Peronnell would be living together in comfortable retirement. He would have to be very careful what he told Albert and Ethel.

Slowly his reputation was growing on the dockside, and he was becoming well known in the port. The old boat owner came down to St. Augustine's Reach whenever he was well enough, and Cedric enjoyed chatting to him. On a few occasions he had come out with Cedric; when he was making his first trip to

South Wales, for example. They also worked closely to maintain the shipping records, which determined the payments due to be paid by Cedric to the owner. Occasionally the old man hinted that he might be ready to sell Fandangle, but though Cedric had still retained most of the money Charles had given him, he did not feel quite ready to commit to such a large purchase.

Increasingly, Cedric felt he would like to see Charles again, but the visits to Bridgewater never seemed to allow time to go out to the mill. Then he found an opportunity to go into Bridgewater a full day before the next load of cloth would be ready. Leaving Fandangle in the care of his deckhand, Cedric hired a horse and rode out to the mill.

Albert recognised him as soon as he came into the yard. "Well, we haven't seen anyone from Salisbury for a year, I don't think. What have you been up to?"

"I've been working a boat out of Bristol for some time and have been into Bridgewater a few times, but till now have not had the time to get out to see you. I was hoping to see Charles here."

"We have not seen nor heard anything. I hoped you might know more than me."

Cedric hardly knew what to think, never mind what he should say.

"He was selling everything off and stopped buying wool, so I think he was going to shut the place down, but he never said what his plans were. He had returned from one of his visits to you, just before he decided to shut everything down."

Albert was silent for a few minutes, clearly unwilling to disclose his late-night conversation with Charles.

"He was here for a few days, going off into Bridgewater or somewhere during the day. Then for three days he didn't come back, till one night he turned up after we had gone to bed. He was here for a few hours, then he was gone before dawn. And that's all I know. Anyhow, come in and see Ethel, I 'spect you could do with something to eat."

The conversation in the house was almost a replica of the one in the yard. Ethel knew no more or, if she did, was unwilling to reveal it.

Cedric listened politely, then after a pause, said,

"I wonder what happened in those three missing days."

Albert nodded. "So do I, zno. Summat not very good."

Cedric returned to Bridgewater with his mind in turmoil and slept poorly.

The cloth was loaded the next morning, and on the tide, he moved out into the Bristol Channel. It was better to keep busy and maintain his routine; there was nothing he could do for Charles.

The weeks passed in a blur, then one day, on the wharf at St Augustine's Reach, Cedric saw a smartly dressed young woman in the company of an older man; Peronell, of course, but she was not with Charles. Cedric was not sure if she had recognised him, till later in the day, when she came aboard Fandangle.

Alone together inside the cabin, they could talk freely.

"Did Charles give any reason for selling up in Salisbury, Nell?"

"No, he arranged for me to leave without anyone seeing me go. He gave me your horse and some cash, but no reason for going, and no clue where he planned to go."

"He did the same for me, though not such a good horse. Anyway, it suited me; I already had this boat lined up."

"It does not suit me at all. I just want to be with Charles. He said he hoped we'd meet again."

If Cedric had heard her deeply wounded response, he was so engrossed with his own thoughts that he seemed to ignore it.

"So, I suppose when he left the mill, he took the last of the finished cloth to the broker in Southampton? He probably went across the water. I wonder if he owed money. That could explain the secrecy."

Nell was still sniffing at the memory of that last dreadful day with Charles.

"Anyway, Nell; you've landed on your feet again. Moving in fine circles, I see."

"I'd give anything to be with Charles, but first I have to survive."

"So, who is the new man?"

"Adam. He is a merchant, I think. He told me his family have been here for three generations."

"Well, find out everything you can about his business. It might come in useful one day. Anyway, you'll often find me tied up here. I'm in and out three or four times a week."

A few days later, Cedric was loading wine when he noticed a young man watching him closely. He touched his hat as a mark of respect, and the man stepped forward to speak to him.

"Where is that wine going?"

"Gloucester. I take some up there most weeks."

"We sell a lot of wine here in Bristol but have never sent any out by water."

He watched patiently as the loading was completed, then asked, "Could I come up to Gloucester with you? We might be able to develop some business there."

Sensing an opportunity, Cedric agreed immediately.

The trip was uneventful, and they arrived in Gloucester before high tide. There was no back load on this occasion, and they came out two hours later with their passenger, making good speed till they reached the mouth of the Avon. Finding some slack water, they anchored up to wait for the next rising tide to carry them up to Bristol. The passenger was not talkative, but while waiting for two hours, someone had to say something. Cedric and his deckhand tidied up the boat and polished a bit of metalwork to pass the time.

Eventually, Cedric decided he must make some attempt to speak. "I come into Bristol three or four times a week, so if you want anything taken up to Gloucester, or across to South Wales, you'll find me on the wharf, as usual."

"Oh, I'm sure we'll be in touch. They seem to be quite interested in a new source of supply."

"I'm going down empty to Bridgewater to bring up a load of cloth tomorrow. I could take some of your wine down and see if I could sell it there, perhaps?"

"Yes, let's try that."

"I'll leave at the top of the tide, about sunrise, and anchor up in Bridgewater Bay till there's enough water to carry me up the Parrett. But I never know how quickly I'll be loaded. The weavers don't have much idea about tides."

He did not add that he might spend some time with Emma while in Bridgewater.

Cedric was provided with a price list for selling the wine and another that he owed to the wine merchant; the difference was his own margin.

"You may have to reduce the selling price to get a sale, but you will be reducing your margin, not mine."

In less than two hours, the wine had been stored safely on board, and the paperwork had been put away in his cabin.

Cedric was exhilarated at the thought of trading on his own account, and the prospect of increasing his income. If this worked out, he could consider buying Fandangle and establish himself as an independent trader.

When he reached Bridgewater, he had time to wait before the cloth arrived, so he smartened himself up a bit and took some of the wine to the nearest alehouse. At first, no one wanted to buy, but after an hour, he achieved his first sale.

Returning to the boat, a publican he had spoken to earlier came up to him. Cedric greeted him with a smile. "I've still got a bit left, if you want to try this out. It comes from a merchant house in Bristol that has been trading for three generations. You won't regret it, and I'll be back in Bridgewater in about three weeks with some more."

This was a cautious man and he only bought two bottles, took them inside, and must have tried the first bottle himself. Later in the day, he came to the boat as they were tying down the load of cloth and purchased two more.

Cedric was so keen to sell all his stock that he missed the next tide. He made his way to the far side of town, where Emma worked, and suggested she might like to spend the night on board. Emma was due for a few days off, so she had a word with her boss, who came out to see Cedric with her.

"So, you are branching out into the wine trade, now?"

"Yes, and I've sold nearly all of it; just got six bottles left."

"This is some good stuff, but it will be wasted on this rabble. I'll just have a couple for myself."

"It comes from a very reliable wine house in Bristol; been there for three generations, you know."

"What price, if I have the six?"

"Well, I can only let you have five. Emma and I will need the other one. But I am on narrow margins; I can only allow a few pence."

They strolled back to the boat, carrying the last bottle. Cedric was almost purring with pleasure. Emma had never seen him so contented, though had not forgotten the ugly side he sometimes showed.

Next morning, they moved very slowly from the dock into the Parrett as the tide turned, winding this way and that; the river full for another hour, then a few inches of mud showing, a small wash from the boat splashing against the bank as Fandangle gained speed. An hour later, they were in Bridgewater Bay, mud banks of peculiar shape growing and changing imperceptibly. Cedric watched intently, keeping as far from the exposed mud as he possibly could.

Then the mud fell behind, and they were out in the Severn with the tide now carrying them away from Bristol; only a light westerly breeze slowing the drift while they moved out into deeper water. All of this was quite new to Emma, and new enough to Cedric to demand his full concentration. A shouted command to the deckhand, and the anchor was thrown overboard. The rope lay slack for several minutes before it snagged, became tight, and swung the boat around.

Cedric turned to Emma and smiled.

"Now we'll wait for the tide to turn."

"I'll make you a drink and find something to eat."

"Well, no rush now, we'll be here for a good while."

Looking back to shore, they could see a large flock of gulls rising and swirling and feasting above the mud flats.

"They go crazy for a while, then when they calm down, you know the tide will not be far from the turn."

Hours later, they stood in the bows together, an accelerating tide and a freshening westerly carrying them to Bristol at increasing speed.

Emma turned to Cedric. "I can see why you love this outdoor life. The slap of the water against the bow is something I never expected."

He looked at her silently, happy in their shared enjoyment.

"Yep, this is the life for me."

"It is nice, but I'd like a garden."

"How about a flowerpot on the cabin roof?"

The approach to Bristol Harbour was slightly unnerving for Emma. The strongly rising tide propelled them through the Avon Gorge quite briskly, though slackened as they approached high tide.

They moved into the wharf area at St. Augustine's Reach, leaving the main flow of the river behind. A rope from the stern of Fandangle was caught skilfully ashore and looped over a bollard. The agile young man moved along the quay to take a second rope from the bow, then waited expectantly for his tip.

"Do you want to unload?"

"I expect I'll have to wait for the buyer," replied Cedric. He knew it paid to treat the wharf boys with consideration.

In the event, the buyer did not arrive till the next day, and it was well after noon before the boat was empty. Cedric had, by this time, settled his account with the wine merchant, to their mutual satisfaction. He suspected his sister, Nell, had prompted this opportunity, and was well disposed towards her when she came aboard later in the day.

He greeted her warmly and remembered to introduce Emma.

"I wonder if you have heard about the new wine distributor in the city, Nell?"

"Well, yes, I knew something about it, and I can see from your face that things must have gone well."

"If I can keep selling the wine, I'll take the chance to buy Fandangle. Things are looking up, I reckon. But I wish I knew how Charles was doing. He's not been seen in Bridgewater the last year."

"So do I, brother dear. So do I." And after an uncomfortable pause, she added, "I suppose I'll just have to keep hoping we'll meet again, as he said."

Nell's eyes were brimming with tears, and Emma moved suddenly to put her arms around her and give her a big hug.

Cedric gazed awkwardly at the floor.

CHAPTER FOURTEEN

Escape to Anonymity.

A travel-weary Englishman came ashore at a small port on the west bank of the River Seine. His face was pale, his walk unsteady, his manner diffident. If anyone cared to watch him, it would be assumed he had endured a bad crossing. On second look, they would have noticed a well-dressed man of later middle age, yet all was not well with him, as his face clearly showed.

The harbour was attractive, framed by warehouses or storage barns in one quarter, and small merchant's houses in another. The cobble stone roads were clean and well maintained. The Englishman noted a boat unloading cloth, with the aid of a simple wooden crane. Two short, sturdy men wound the handle of the crane till the bale of un-dyed English broadcloth was clear of the deck. Then, with the aid of two more men, they swung the crane around till it was hanging over a simple oxcart. When the load was secure, the oxen were driven to the rear of one of the storage barns. The creatures were cursed at loudly in an alien language, though there was something familiar in the tone of voice, suggesting impatience and anger. Charles supposed the words were as brutal and profane as the English equivalents.

He thought he might engage the boat's crew in conversation but knew better than to interfere while they were busy with this crucial and slightly dangerous work. Instead, he made his way slowly and carefully into the town, where he hoped he might exchange his English cash for whatever coin might be used here. Then, and only then, he might eat and find lodgings.

Charles woke with the sun the following day. He had dined lightly on soup and remarkably fresh bread before bed. Then, after a prayer for the safety and comfort of his lost love, he slept deeply. Now, somewhat restored after the lightest imaginable breakfast, he ventured forth to explore the town. The morning air was crisp and the tang of the sea invigorating. For the first time in many weeks, he felt no threat of exposure, reassured by the incomprehensible babble of conversation around him.

Charles found he could make himself understood by talking very slowly and pointing at objects he might wish to buy. Listening carefully, he soon picked up a few useful phrases, though finding suitable cheap accommodation was impossible until he was helped by a bi-lingual native. Slowly, over many weeks, he developed the ability to express himself in limited phrases, but rarely understood the replies.

Occasionally, Charles heard an English voice, though was unsure if he should make himself known, so waited till someone spoke to him directly.

Alone in his room, his thoughts often tuned to Nell, and the agony of not knowing if she was safe and well. He hoped she was safe with her family at White Clyffe, but knew her pain and sorrow would be no less than his own. What chance they would ever meet again?

Charles became aware of a small colony of English-speaking people in Honfleur, one of whom had been active during the wild and heady weeks of the Peasants' Revolt a while earlier. Indeed, Charles had arranged his safe passage through Southampton. Though there was a sense of security in a foreign country, neither spoke of their involvement within earshot of anyone from the English community.

Charles was able to bring news of the gradual return to normal, though his recent experience of arrest and interrogation in Bridgewater was cause for anxiety. The chance of a safe return to England seemed a remote prospect.

Gradually it became apparent that the English community consisted of displaced people, most of whom had left England because of debts, disgrace, or fear of revenge. Just occasionally, a younger adventurer might settle among them for the ease and convenience of the common tongue. But sooner rather than later, the flakiness, the air of dissolution, and the dispiriting scruffiness of the community encouraged the younger optimists to move away to the south, usually to Paris.

Charles obtained work when his French improved sufficiently to enable him to manage a conversation. His first job was to teach businessmen the finer points of the English language, most usefully to those with a basic understanding of English. The school, if that is not too grand a description of the training establishment, was managed by a small, energetic lady of uncertain age. Her partner, perhaps husband, was rarely present, and usually returned late, when industrious people were already abed. Nor was he seen before mid-day, in the normal course of events. When he left the house, he carried a large flat bag or satchel that might contain tasteful sketches of the coastline, or perhaps plans of ambitious proposals for a fine workshop. In reality, no one knew his purpose or function, except perhaps Madame.

Charles was learning as he taught, and within a few months, could share a conversation with Madame. He was instinctively obliging and considerate, and quite commonly, spent an hour after the students had left, cleaning and tidying the premises. Madame was sometimes sufficiently grateful to invite him to share a glass of wine with her. Their conversations ranged wider than his day-to-day minimum survival requirements. Yes, he could buy a stick of bread or a beer, but Madame might discuss music or the theatre, or recent events in Honfleur. Charles understood that this would open up social opportunities and was happy to listen. Gradually he might offer opinions.

The conversations grew longer, but Charles never remained long enough to meet Madame's partner on his eventual return.

The winter nights in Honfleur were no warmer than those of southern England, and a chill north-easterly from the sea would cut him to the bone. One day, Madame suggested taking him into town to help him buy a suitable coat for the winter. Charles was touched by her concern, but the experience reminded him too vividly of the day he had taken Nell to buy smart clothes in Salisbury, scarcely a year earlier. Later, he bought Madame lunch, and this they enjoyed together while his mood lightened visibly. At one point they even laughed together at some silly verbal mistake he had made.

Charles escorted Madame to her home quite slowly, chatting easily. Madame opened the front door and left it open. Charles hesitated, then followed her in. On her own ground, Madame became more confident,

"I saw you were unhappy when choosing the clothes, Charles."

"Yes, it reminded me of a painful episode in England."

"Do you want to talk about this?"

"It is still quite difficult."

"Your face told me that, but let us hope that time, and maybe distance, will help you heal."

Charles smiled gratefully but moved the conversation to safer ground. He thanked Madame for her help, and there were plans for some changes he wanted to suggest for the next week. The moment of intimacy had passed.

The weeks became months and spring ultimately arrived, then, as if by magic, the warmer weather brought out brightly coloured clothes; even Madame shed a few layers. She carried a parasol to protect her skin from the sun, still free from wrinkles; a compliment was received elegantly. Charles found her company refreshing after the limited conversations among the male-only English community.

One afternoon, when the school had closed for the day, Charles politely enquired after Madame's health, but the reply was non-committal.

"And your husband, is he also well?"

"Who do you mean? I have no husband. You cannot think that I might have married that clumsy, social misfit who lives in the attic?"

Charles apologised and agreed it had seemed surprising.

After a pause, Madame said, "I must treat my skin. The sun is so damaging."

As she moved to go to her quarters, Charles watched her walk away with the swish of a long dress and a slight sway of the hips he was sure he had not seen before.

Later that evening, when he was sitting at a street café with a few members of the English community, his mind wandered back to the swaying hips of Madame. He had been stroking the stem of his wine glass lingeringly when his thoughts were interrupted.

"Who are you dreaming about, Charles? A thirsty man does not play with a wine glass like that."

He was relieved by the chorus of laughter that saved him from responding. Charles was not a great contributor to the general conversation, so little was expected of him. Some of the younger ones moved away to see what might be happening in the town. Soon, only Charles and his former ally from the disturbances in Salisbury remained.

"Why do you think you were pulled in after so many years, Charles?"

"Well, I can't be sure, but a group of us were in an alehouse talking about the need for change in the villages."

"That was a bit risky, wasn't it?"

"With hindsight, yes it was. But we were only talking about making better use of the wasteland, which would have grown wheat thirty years ago, when we were young. And we did discuss it with the stewards, so there was no threat."

"Did they rough you up?"

"Yes, they did, for three days and nights. They did not believe what I was saying. I suppose they fear another organised rebellion."

His friend was silent for a while, then after a heavy sigh, said, "I was hoping to return to

England again, but now I don't know if I'll ever be safe there."

"Perhaps you could go to one of those districts where there was no trouble, or change your name, perhaps. What would you like? Jacques? Francois? Anyway, we'd better have another drink; we don't want to go to bed in a morbid state of mind. And there is quite a lot to like about this place."

*　　　*　　　*

During the long days of summer, fears of royal revenge seemed more distant. Evening walks with Madame in the cooler air, laden with a fragrance from unfamiliar shrubs, were a delight. The anxious, fretful Charles had mellowed during many weeks of long lunches and somnolent afternoons.

Madame's gentle care brought peace of mind, but her manners were impeccable, and he was naturally somewhat reserved. Neither could manage the tender touch or sympathetic gesture that would allow the friendship to develop. The conversation was usually circumspect, reflecting perhaps on a recent visit to the theatre, or a choral concert. Only once, and quite by chance, Madame had been exasperated by the behaviour of the strange man in the attic. Charles had wondered aloud why she had permitted him to stay.

"The school was founded by his mother, and in her later years, she worried how her son might manage when he was alone. He had lived in the attic for many years, from a time before I arrived to teach here. In her later years, the old lady, his mother, became too tired to teach."

Charles listened politely but made no comment. Madame thought her explanation had been incomplete, and after the briefest pause, continued, "Eventually she was unable even to manage the school, and these things all passed naturally to me. Over the course of time, she also passed the school itself to me, and I agreed to care for her son, but the building belongs to him."

After a few moments, Charles asked, "Do you have family here in the town?"

Madame paused before replying, and he knew he had probed too far into her past.

"No, not in Honfleur."

Neither spoke for several minutes. Then Charles said there was much to like about Honfleur.

"Yes, of course. It is quite charming. But you must miss your people in England. Is that not so?"

"There are people in England I care for, and one person I miss profoundly."

"I had already sensed that was so."

They both became aware that the sun had gone. Already the temperature had changed.

Charles rose to his feet. "Thank you, Madame, for your hospitality, but the light is fading, and I must be on my way."

"Yes, of course, Charles. Thank you for your company."

A few days later, after the pupils had left the school, Charles made his way to the port. It was the day of the market, and he might find a few bargains late in the day, before the traders removed their stalls. Sometimes an opportunistic trader might set up on the hard when fishing boats returned, which always drew a crowd, but today there were no fishermen, only an English freighter sitting on the mud. The crew were waiting aimlessly for the tide to raise the boat before they could off-load. But two men, standing apart from the crew, had very alert appearances and were studying the market and the buildings near the port. They had the air of men with a sense of purpose; perhaps frustrated at having to wait for the tide.

Charles noted them briefly, but his attention was soon taken by a stallholder with some off-cuts of cheese that would suit him if the price were not so high. A conversation dominated by the stallholder established the remarkable merits and the source of the original cheese he had brought in from the countryside just that morning. Only because he was preparing to return could he make Charles an offer which he must agree was a gift. Charles responded with an offer of his own, to the horror of the stall holder.

"But how will the people on the farm live through the winter on such a small sum? Have a care, sir, for the poor and unfortunate."

But the stallholder was losing patience and wanted to clear up at the end of a long day. Weakly protesting, he lowered his price, and Charles accepted.

When Charles looked again, the two men had gone below, though the crew still lazed comfortably in the afternoon sun. He found some fresh bread and returned with the cheese to his room to enjoy a late lunch and a well-earned sleep.

The next time he passed the port, the English freighter had gone, replaced by two empty fishing boats sitting high in the water. From time to time, Charles bumped into friends from the English community, usually joining them for a drink. Sometimes a stranger joined them, or one of the businessmen from the school.

Life in Honfleur was really quite pleasant, and if Nell had only accompanied him, he felt he might settle here peacefully. Each night he prayed for her happiness and her safety. He simply did not know what to think about her situation.

Most days, after the school had closed, Charles would make his way to a café in Honfleur for a glass of wine and a lazy conversation before taking an afternoon nap. From time to time, the regulars of the English community would walk by the café, pausing to chat long enough with Charles to assess the possibility of a free glass of wine. Charles was closer to his old colleague from the mad days of the Peasants' Revolt and had felt a little disappointed that he had not seen him for a few days. When he asked around, he gradually discovered that no one else had seen him either. His heart sank when he realised that his friend's disappearance had coincided with the arrival of the two sinister passengers on the small English freighter in the harbour at Honfleur. They had not come over by chance; they had been too alert, their eyes searching, and they knew what they wanted.

This was sickening. They may come again. Indeed, if his friend talked, under interrogation, they would have all the information they needed to identify Charles. Perhaps he should move along the coast or get on a boat leaving the harbour.

For the next few days, Charles visited the harbour on every tide, sometimes chatting to the crew to find out when they would be leaving and gain some indication of their intended destination. Often, the sailors had no knowledge and were less interested in their next voyage, provided they were fed, housed, and paid.

Charles decided he would have to talk to the skippers directly and, in time, found one who was prepared to take a passenger, though he would be leaving before the tide turned.

Charles hurried home, collected his belongings, tidied his room, closed the door quietly, and slipped away without speaking to anyone.

CHAPTER FIFTEEN

Sleepy Days.

Meanwhile, at Bridgewater, the town slumbered in a late summer drought, busy if busy at all, with the daily routine of regular work. Twice each day the tide came in, drowning the mudflats of Bridgewater Bay, and twice each day it receded. On some days, small freighters or fishing boats made it to the harbour wall, while on others, no one called.

A few miles to the west of the town, the mill, now in the hands of Charles' wife Ethel, was still managed by Albert, as it had been for most of his adult life. But the mill could not operate for want of water in the stream that drove the mill, and Albert struggled to find useful work for the cloth workers. A few had returned to their families to help with the wheat harvest and, for once, farmers were in good humour at the busiest time of the farming year.

The opportunity was taken to strip some of the thatch from one of the barns that leaked pitifully after every good storm. Albert had been offended by the squalid conditions in this barn for so long, but he was in high spirits to be able to set it to rights. An experienced thatcher, he had learned the trade, like most men in the village, thatching small ricks of hay in mid-summer, then larger stacks of wheat as harvest progressed. Within a few months, the thatch was removed as the hay was taken for the cattle or the wheat threshed for bread-making.

The thatching straw protected the precious contents for such a short period that the utilitarian mind might dismiss the need for craftmanship, but it only needed one thatcher to trim the ridge of the roof to set off the competition; another would trim the eaves and, pretty soon, it became the standard. It was only a matter of time before the body of thatcher's decorated their work with straw dollies, each one an individual signature of their work.

Special pride was taken with the thatching of buildings that might stand beyond the end of a man's life, even a humble storage barn in a clothier's mill-yard. Albert took one of his trusted young men, with experience of rick thatching since childhood. "Now, Johnnie, I'm gonna start you off, and when you've got it going right, I'll leave you to it." Though Johnnie and everyone in the yard knew that his beady eye would be scanning the barn roof at every opportunity.

The thatch was prepared from the straw of threshed wheat, combed, and sorted by hand to remove short and broken lengths of straw. Laid carefully in small bundles known as yelms, they were tied together in a large but manageable bundle to be carried up the long ladder when the thatcher called.

At the end of a long day, young Johnnie came down the ladder with care, for un-used muscles in his back reminded him of unaccustomed frailty.

Albert asked, "Are you happy with the roof, then?"

"Yea, I think it is going all right."

Albert simply nodded his approval.

Albert and Ethel took their evening meal in the garden when the long summer evenings made this possible. The meal was washed down with a cold cider from the cellar. Albert stretched out his legs in satisfaction,

"Johnnie have done a good job today."

"You have been looking at that roof all evening. You'd better sit with your back to it, before you ruin your digestion."

"I be pleased to make a start on thic job, thee 'ould know."

"I know that well enough, and you have grumbled about it for years."

They might have been an old married couple, completely at ease together, and indeed they had long been together, though each had different memories of Charles.

After a long pause, Albert said, "I hope he would be happy to see the improvement. I'd like to think he'll call in to see it one day, wherever he is now."

Ethel did not respond at once but was lost in her own thoughts for quite some time. Then, after a sigh, she said, "All I know is he is not here, but you are."

Much later, in bed together, Ethel ran her fingertips along Albert's forearm. "I be glad you are here, but you know that, I'm sure."

Chapter Sixteen

The Search for Charles.

Nell was currently escorting a former Lord Mayor of Bristol and using his town flat as her home. He was never the most generous of patrons, but he was a kindly man and needed a social companion for some events; he dressed her well and there had been a few nice jewels now safely stored against a rainy day. There were younger admirers, but she never permitted any of them to know her arrangements and was quite clear that no one should return to the town flat, they must provide their own safe accommodation.

While she enjoyed the attention of younger men, she was careful not to become involved. Young men could soon become possessive. She learned to detect the danger signs and usually detached herself in good time. Despite her care and precautions an ugly scene developed when she was walking with her patron to attend a major event in the city. Two men who accompanied him for security dealt with the passionate young man and they continued to the dinner without anyone being the wiser. However, the young man did not recover from his injuries. An investigation led to unfavourable publicity and after unpleasant arguments Nell decided to leave Bristol for a while.

Cedric travelled with her to White Clyffe, and she was pleased to see her family again. Her father was still fully alert though her mother seemed not to recognise her, nor Cedric. Cedric could not remain long and left early on the second morning; he could not afford to leave his boat sitting idle. Her younger brothers were cheerful but there was simply not enough common ground and conversations petered out into silence. Her younger sister had married and was completely pre-occupied with a small baby. It was apparently too fragile to be entrusted to a clumsy older sister.

On market day Nell walked into Calne market taking care to dress down. There she met her cousins who were busy with the market stall; they were pleased to have an extra pair of hands and Nell was relieved to have some work to do. When she returned to White Clyffe she told her father she would help the cousins again and might live with them for convenience, though would return as often as possible. She soon got into the rhythm of attending local markets and when the time came to take the wagon to Salisbury for supplies, she went too.

While in the city she remembered a conversation with Cedric when he suggested Charles would have taken his last loads of cloth to the broker in Southampton, then when all the payments had been settled; he might well have set sail for France. On an impulse she bought a horse and rode to Southampton. After a short search she found the broker and introduced herself as the sister of Cedric; the owner who remembered Cedric quite well was delighted to meet her.

"I have come here to trace my friend Charles who brought his last loads of cloth to you nearly two years ago."

"Come through to my office and we'll look at the records."

He nodded his head and confirmed there had been six loads in a few weeks. "I presume he was selling up the business?"

"That is what my brother thinks, but I don't know, he never told me what was happening. He just gave me a horse and some money and told me to ride back to my family at White Clyffe."

Nell struggled to speak as the memories overwhelmed her. The broker was silent while she recovered. One last big sniff and she started again,

"Do you have any idea where I should start looking for him?"

"I've not seen him since that time, nor do I know anyone in the cloth trade who has, so I think he must have taken a ship to somewhere ...... possibly France."

Without hesitation Nell asked, "Can you find me a boat going to France that will take me and my horse?"

The crossing was stormy, and the skipper was blown off-course; huge waves broke over the bows of the flat-bottomed boat and there was no relief for Nell or her new horse. After a long night and a grey dawn there seemed no prospect of improvement; lashed by rain and seawater driven by fierce squalls, endurance levels of crew and passengers were severely tested.

A dim smudge of something that might have been land, offered a slight hope of relief and as the hours passed it became clear the boat was moving closer to the shore. Coming close enough to see the detail it became evident they were circling around a small island. Perhaps the skipper was searching for a possible harbour, but if so, he was to be disappointed. However, he did manage to hold the boat in sheltered seas avoiding the worst of the wind. The next day was much more comfortable and though the island was left behind, they were soon in sight of land again. Yet wherever it was, it was many miles from the intended destination, but no matter, for there was a harbour, and the boat had stopped heaving.

A blessed peace settled over the passengers as soon as the boat was secured to the wharf, though another adjustment was needed to enable them to walk on solid land. The horse was led ashore carefully, and Nell made no attempt to ride her till the next day. Attempts to make contact with the people of the small town or village where they had landed were defeated by a mutual lack of understanding, till someone thought to ask the Priest to intervene.

He had some knowledge of English though had not practised speaking the language for almost twenty years. Slowly and gradually an understanding was achieved, but the priest was extremely anxious for Nell's safety, if she should ride alone through sparsely populated countryside.

He suggested she wait for a few weeks to join a group of his parishioners who were making a pilgrimage to the cathedral in a much larger town where there may be an English group of people. It would be a few weeks before they would leave, but if she cared to help the Priest in his church, he could arrange for her to live with his other helpers.

Working with the village women was in sharp contrast to her recent life of luxury among the wealthiest men of Bristol. Nell was thankful for her upbringing on the small dairy farm at White Clyffe where she had been accustomed to menial tasks.

She could not avoid noticing that a surprising number of sturdy young men were drawn to the Church. Perhaps the Priest was a popular preacher in the village, though it would be a long time before she would be able to appreciate his dramatic gifts. Most of the young men were considerate and much given to smiling, so she felt she must smile in return. Heads too, were often nodded in the absence of effective conversation.

The working women were quite jolly by comparison, loud and spontaneous in their conversation which Nell could often follow by watching their actions and reactions. The women were amused by the earnest young men, though only revealed this after they had disappeared. One of the working women was a capable mime and produced a remarkable imitation of the most persistent young men to general delight. Nell responded by placing her hands in solemn prayer then extended her forefinger to draw a halo over her head. This produced a roar of laughter, an emphatic shaking of the head, followed by a gesture indicating a beating heart. Another woman took it a stage further and with her forearm and clenched fist mimed an erect male penis, though some of the women were hesitant to laugh till they saw Nell's enjoyment of the joke.

As the weeks passed Nell began to feel anxious and frustrated. After six weeks she was no closer to meeting anyone who might have known Charles. She must talk to the Priest who had not been seen for a while. Days passed before he re-appeared, a benign smile seemed slightly fixed, and his eyes were tired. He had been walking from village to village for weeks and had brought about a dozen people of various ages who had been persuaded to make a pilgrimage to the great cathedral; most were women.

After a busy Sunday, a group formed outside the parish church at the beginning of the week and were brought in for a divine blessing. They were commencing a risky and potentially dangerous journey; there would be exhaustion and there would be hunger, but he encouraged them to place their trust in God's Hands. Nell was surprised that no one knew which way they should travel but relied entirely on the priest's ability to find the Cathedral City; if he should fall ill or worse, they would all be lost in an unknown district.

Only Nell had a horse, but she felt she must walk alongside the others, though in any case the horse was loaded up with a supply of necessities for a venture of unknown distance or duration. As the days and nights passed the pilgrims developed their begging techniques and formed a new admiration for the Priest's nerve and brass-faced determination. Rations were sparse; twenty-six stomachs could not be fed satisfactorily by a few good-natured people in tiny villages and simple farms. As the weeks passed most of the pilgrims tired visibly. Their walking pace declined to a feeble shuffling gait. Then the road swung closer to the shore and their spirits were lifted a little by the invigorating smell of the sea. For two days and three nights they rested on the seashore. The Priest and the strongest among the walkers went out foraging and begging and for a few days these meagre supplies were supplemented by fresh fish from the sea.

When the Priest returned on the second day, he told Nell they were only a day's walk from a seaport where, he had been told, there was a group of English people. They may well have knowledge of Nell's friend. However, the route to the cathedral city lay to the south-east so their route would diverge. Nell had grown attached to the faithful group and their spirt of mutual help and kindness. Still the possibility of meeting someone with news of Charles whereabouts lifted her spirits and overcame her sadness.

At first light they parted with good natured farewells. Nell mounted her horse for the first time in many weeks, waved the pilgrims goodbye for the last time and trotted out of sight. Late in the day she reached the port quite stiff from unaccustomed riding. She found there was an attractive harbour with storage barns in one quarter and some small merchant's houses not far removed.

A number of people moved around the harbour and the trader's stalls. She felt sufficiently confident of her French to ask if anyone could speak English, but only one stall holder responded. She bought some bread and cheese and ate ravenously, oblivious of the attention of the people watching her. One of these asked her if it was good. "Oui, oui, tres bien," she responded with a smile and her questioner was captivated. Haltingly she attempted to explain her search for an older Englishman called Charles. Slowly she learned there was a small English community in the town, but first she must find lodging for the night.

The next day she hoped she might meet someone who could speak English, but people seemed to be busy at work when she emerged from her lodgings. If they had started the day with the modest breakfast she had been offered, she could only admire their willpower and stamina. Only when the sun was at the highest point would they stop for what proved to be an extended meal, the bowl splashed with fine red wine when empty, then wiped clean with successive pieces of bread, each sucked with relish.

The cafes continued to be busy through the evening, people moving slowly with glass or mug in hand, chatting easily to complete strangers and this is how she found her first Englishman. Though there were three to be more exact. How easy it was to talk English again after so many weeks of mental effort.

She was offered a glass of wine by a pleasant young man,

"Or would you prefer cider? It's just as good as the stuff from Somerset."

Nell laughed easily and said she would give it a try.

"Well, I have drunk nothing but wine for weeks, it'll be nice for a change."

Conversation was easy and she soon mentioned her search for Charles. None of them knew anyone of that name. She described him as best she could, though did not know when he arrived in France or indeed if he had ever been in this town or any other. One member of the group did mention there were other English people in the town, and they met from time to time, perhaps someone else might know something.

She met the English people most evenings but only after at least a week of fruitless enquiries was she given any hope or clue that she could follow. The conversation turned to learning the French language and from there to Frenchmen learning the English language. Someone had heard there was once an Englishman who taught in a language school in the town, though no one knew who he was or if he was still teaching. Nell immediately wanted to know where she might find the language school, but no one amongst the group had been in the town long enough to know where to find it.

The next day she asked for directions to the language school but mostly was met with an expressive shrug of the shoulders. She began to worry that the school had closed or failed and returned to her lodgings where the owner's daughter was visiting from Paris to be with the family. The daughter knew there had been a language school and furthermore knew of someone who had once used it to improve his language skills. Later in the evening she returned to say she had discovered the location and would take Nell there tomorrow in daylight.

When they found the school, Madame was unable to see them but arranged a time later in the day. Having explored the town and the harbour while they were waiting, Nell and her new friend returned for their appointment. The conversation was entirely in French, and Nell was quite unable to follow what Madame was saying. Her voice had been unemotional, her face severe, so when they walked away Nell was astonished to learn from her friend that an Englishman name Charles had worked there for almost a year but could not say where he went or even if he was still in Honfleur.

Having found someone who could confirm that Charles had been there till quite recently, Nell desperately wanted to know if he had been well or ill, sad or happy. Almost despite herself she walked past the language school on the next day at about the time Madame had agreed to see them. If Madame was looking out of the windows, she chose not to come out to speak to Nell, nor again on the next day.

On the third day Nell was a little later, and on this occasion, she met Madame walking into town; they paused in the shade of a large tree. Madame now spoke in English so had understood Nell's conversation with her friend two days earlier. On this occasion she was friendly and sympathetic and assured Nell that Charles had become more relaxed as time passed, though it was clear to her that he missed her acutely.

"He will not be happy till you are together again, I think."

Nell's face was lit with gratitude, and she held her face in her hands trying not to weep with relief.

CHAPTER SEVENTEEN

Together in Bristol.

Nell returned to Southampton, struggling to deal with conflicting emotions of relief and torment. Knowing how Charles had spent the year after he had left England gave her something tangible to cling to, and for Madame to assure her that Charles missed her was heart-warming. Then again, where did he go, and why did he leave suddenly, without saying goodbye or giving an explanation to Madame, who had treated him so kindly? This new puzzle was a second torture.

After a night in Southampton, Nell rode to Salisbury, taking lodgings for a few days until her cousins arrived for their regular buying trips, seeking better quality goods than could be found in the little market towns of north Wiltshire. The cousins were relieved and delighted to see her after so many months, particularly because they had not yet told Nell's father she might be in France.

The journey back to her childhood home was a sentimental relief. The well-trodden road along the Avon valley to Upavon, and later the views across the cultivated Vale of Pewsey, sheltering beneath the rugged grandeur of the Marlborough Downs, provided the comfort of familiarity.

Her father was delighted to see her once more, though astonished to learn that she had been to France, searching for a 'friend'.

"Must have been a very close friend, I'd say. And did you find him?"

At the sight of Nell's tragic face, he put his arm around her shoulders.

"Oh, Dad, I didn't," and she laid her wet cheeks against his leathery old skin.

After a short stay with her father, Nell's cousins were kind enough to accompany her to Bristol; partly for her protection, but also because they wondered what possibilities for trade might be there. They were greatly excited to see Cedric again and joined him on a trip upriver to Gloucester.

The hours on the boat passed quickly, with the novelty of the ports along the upper Severn and the sights of life along the riverbanks displaying such a contrast to their routine journeys between the small towns of Wiltshire. The return to Bristol was a bit rougher and their country stomachs reacted violently, reminding Cedric of his early days at sea. The cousins left Fandangle thinking there was something to be said for journeys on dry land.

The years in Bristol had been good for Cedric. He had made steady progress with Fandangle and purchased the boat from the old owner. His supplementary income selling wine, alongside his routine deliveries of wheat, cloth or Irish fish, had also boosted his income. He was always busy on the wharf and had developed a wide range of business contacts.

Boats arrived and departed on every tide; visitors came down from the city to see the activity. Among the throng of working boat crews, passengers coming or leaving, a figure disembarked from a boat that had just arrived from Ireland. Cedric was waiting to be loaded nearby and saw a stooped figure coming ashore but did not give it a second thought. Later, the same man made his way along the wharf just as Cedric went down the gang plank, and he paused to let the older gentleman pass by. When he turned towards him, his face lit up in recognition.

"Cedric, isn't it? Good to see you again!"

They held hands for a long moment, then Cedric said, "Come aboard, will you, Charles?"

Cedric was careful not to give any details of Nell's activities but decided to talk to her and arrange a meeting on his boat. But while Cedric was out in the Channel, Charles bumped into Nell in a crowded street. Both wanted to throw their arms around the other, but there were too many people watching. They were exhilarated to be together again, though Nell was cautious in public. Before they parted, Nell managed to say that they should meet on Cedric's boat.

Through her contacts, Nell was able to find accommodation for Charles not far from the wharf. She visited Charles in his attic room whenever she could, sometimes helping him down the narrow stairs when his knees were stiff. It took a little while for his eyes to become accustomed to bright sunlight, but the warmth of the sun and the sweetness of the air lifted his mood immediately. They would stroll to the wharf when he felt up to it, but soon he would look for a bench to rest his bones, or perhaps he might take a low stone wall. Sometimes, but only rarely, she might meet someone who recognised her, and she was immediately pleased to introduce her Uncle Charles. He, in turn, carried the deception off gracefully, his concise diction and social confidence reinforced Nell's own impression of class and good taste. Since arriving in Bristol, he had a tailor make his clothes in the current style, and they made a charming couple.

The wharf was always busy, with small boats alongside larger boats from the continent. But the high point was always the sight of Fandangle entering the harbour, with Cedric concentrating carefully, and usually making a good arrival. The boat safely moored, the crew were instructed to scrub down the decks and have her looking her best. Then Cedric would come ashore and greet them both.

"Well, how are you, Charles? You are looking well, you know."

"I am doing my best, but I'll never be able to compete with lovely Nell, I don't suppose."

Over the last few years, Nell had understood her precarious position and put money and jewels away for a rainy day; the surface charm concealing a careful hoarder. She was worried her treasures might not be safe in her lodgings in Bristol, so she had spoken to Cedric. He had a secure locked box under his bunk but warned her not to put it all in one place. Another admirer suggested a secure bank safe deposit, perhaps two banks.

Charles' health seemed to be deteriorating, and Nell began to worry that city air was not good for him. Charles had a cottage in Ireland and was also becoming anxious that he should return before the rent was due and the owner decided to let it to anyone else.

So, after some weeks of infrequent meetings and frustrating separations, Nell decided to join Charles on a trip to Ireland. Away from the city, the slower pace of life did seem to help Charles. He was noticeably more relaxed, and no longer had attacks where he was fighting for breath. Now they were together in a country where they were unknown and could just be together and stroll along the road hand in hand. People were friendly, and conversation in Ireland was easy.

During their quiet times together, they reminisced about their life in Salisbury, and talked about Honfleur and Madame. Charles explained his sudden departure when his friend and ally from the Peasants' Revolt had disappeared from Honfleur in strange circumstances. He had known immediately that he must go at once and leave no traces. Under interrogation, his friend might have given information that could incriminate Charles and his contacts in Bridgewater.

Gradually, they made the little Irish house more comfortable, and together they collected a store of firewood against the winter. Charles looked at the condition of the house before winter and knew that the thatch really needed repair but felt it would see him out.

*   *   *

Nell returned to Bristol and lived in the city for several weeks before she met Cedric again. She was smartly dressed for social life and, at first sight, she was her old, vivacious self, but even Cedric could see the strain in her face. Yet somehow there was a sense of acceptance. She knew she had given Charles a year of deep contentment and done everything humanly possible to make him comfortable and happy.

As time passed, she was able to talk more easily about Charles' last weeks; how he had slipped away quietly. There had been a nice funeral, attended by most of the people in the village, and before leaving, she had made a payment to the priest to ensure that his grave was well maintained.

Cedric was out in the Bristol Channel twice or three times a week, and meetings with Nell were infrequent.

Before a month had passed, he was making the tricky entrance into Bridgewater, watching for the mud banks like a hawk. On this occasion, he gave himself time to visit Ethel and Albert at the cloth mill, to tell them that Charles had died.

Ethel asked if Charles had been alone.

"No, he was with my sister."

"Were they close?"

Cedric wanted to say that it had been an intense relationship, punctuated by intolerable separations, but could only nod dumbly.

Later, as Cedric was leaving, Albert accompanied him to the stable, thanking Cedric for coming to see them and giving them the news of Charles' death.

"He was a good man to me, and I am glad he did not die alone."

Cedric was relieved to escape from the mill and return to Bridgewater, buoyed by the hope that he might see Emma again. It had been quite a few months since they had been together. She was working that evening but came with him to the boat later. He suggested she might like to have a few days with him in Bristol, but she declined.

"I am going back to my mother for a couple of days to see my daughter. It is her birthday, so I can't miss that. Maybe the next time you come in; I could get some time off?"

Cedric shrugged his shoulders but said little. Gradually, Emma coaxed him into better humour, and something resembling a smile fluttered briefly across his face. Later, they lay peacefully together, stirred later in the night, murmured gently and slept again.

Hours later, the boat, loaded with cloth and tied down, left Bridgewater on the turn of the tide; then there was the familiar slow drift into Bridgewater Bay, and the hours at anchor waiting for the turn.

Now Fandangle is well under way, heading for Bristol on the incoming tide. Cedric stands, a hand on the tiller, legs apart, sensing the boat through the soles of his feet. The boat is alive, and by God, so is he.

This is where he belongs, breathing in the Atlantic air, hair blowing in the wind. Only the tide is his mistress now, and a terrible, implacable mistress she is.

Also by Colin Fletcher…

White Clyffe.

Chapter Three. The Steward.

But almost 400ft above this mayhem, the glorious spire of the cathedral stood serenely, new stonework gleaming, demonstrating the superiority and grandeur of the church. For all the novelty John had encountered on this journey nothing compared remotely with Salisbury Cathedral whose majesty seemed to restore his religious belief.

Chapter Seven. Edith the Market Trader.

Devizes was a new town, like Salisbury, and had only grown up around the building of the Norman Castle … the working people seemed to lack confidence and carried a respectful air of deference. The contrast with Calne was marked, Calne was still a Saxon town to its bones and the townspeople knew their worth.

Chapter Nine. A Wandering Priest.

The tender care from Jenny restored the priest's spirits and he encouraged her to kneel beside his bed in prayer while he stroked her hair softly. The clothier's wife grew suspicious of these absences ... and was only slightly mollified to find Jenny kneeling on the floor, a little too close to the priest for the reputation of a decent household; the next morning the Priest departed.

Chapter Eleven. A Missing Nephew.

Suddenly they heard shouting, six horses abreast burst through a passive crowd of onlookers, through them and over them; a boy kicked in the head by an iron shod foot, died within the hour. Somewhere deep within the city, the spymaster was taking a firm line with one of the spies who reported to him, but the information was stale, not worth a shilling. "Find the old woman and her family and I'll give you five shillings."

READER'S RESPONSE

Please respond to: colin@foxhangers.co.uk

Dear Reader,

Thank you for choosing to read King's Mercy, a sequel to White Clyffe, following the characters we met in the earlier novel; the younger generation of the Johnson family or Charles the clothier, who still felt threatened even when he had escaped to Honfleur.

You may wish to visit our website at colinfletcherauthor. com for Foxhanger's background and news of publishing progress.

Book publishing is a new experience for me, but I am learning fast and am already sure that the most valuable information will be your views and experiences.

After spending six months writing a book, it is quite difficult to place myself in the position of someone who has picked it up and read it for the first time. Your first impressions will be extremely interesting to me.

All suggestions for improvement will be most helpful. Naturally, I hope your experience was enjoyable, but if not, I need to know that too.

Thank you for your response.

Best regards,

Colin Fletcher.

COMING SOON

SOUTHERN WATERS is a story of three canals across southern England. The Kennet & Avon threatened by total abandonment in 1955 was only saved by the founding activists within the Inland Waterways Association who inspired a parliamentary revolt, which succeeded in overturning a government decision to abandon the greatest canal in the south.

The physical recovery of the K&A inspired the next major east-west route across southern England, comprising the Thames & Severn and Stroudwater canals; these connect the upper Thames above Lechlade with the Sharpness Canal beside the Severn leading to the west midland canals.

The gap between the two canal systems will be completed by the Wilts & Berks Canal, a narrow canal originally carrying coal into north Wiltshire, then extended across the Vale of the White Horse to Abingdon on the upper Thames to by-pass the treacherous waters of the upper river. After twenty years of operation the North Wilts canal was cut from the small town of Swindon to connect to the Thames & Severn near its eastern end. Collectively these canals have become known as the Wessex Waterways Network.

Author's warning: this is not an official history of the Wilts & Berks Canal nor of the Wessex Waterways Concept, it is instead a personal journey, a cheerful obsession, a story of friendship and a salute to the volunteer canal restorer. Opinions and comments can only be attributed to the author and may not necessarily coincide with Trust policy.

Colin Fletcher, Foxhangers, April 2022.

CPSIA information can be obtained
at www.ICGtesting.com
Printed in the USA
LVHW111305290722
724664LV00004B/57

9 781803 810621